THE
MURDER
OF
HITLER

AUGUST FRANZA

ISBN: 0-7596-8058-2

This book is printed on acid free paper.

1stBooks - rev. 01/04/02

Chapter One

Franz Kafka had a dream that his sisters were in danger. They were besieged by a machine, but he could not make out what kind of a machine it was. His parents, as usual, were not at home, so he was his sisters' lone defender.

The machine, which rumbled and shrieked, had one occupant and he sat on top of it. He was a thin man with dark hair and he did not seem as tall as Franz. There was an expression on his face that seemed empty of feeling. As he directed the machine forward, it made an awful noise on the Zeltnergasse.

Kafka's sisters noticed it first. Hearing their screams, he jumped out of bed and went to the window which he always kept open regardless of the weather. The machine came rolling down the street frightening his sisters who were cowering in the doorway of a butcher shop. The rest of the pedestrians went about their business as if everything were normal.

"Ottla! Elli! Valli!" Franz called. "Come in the house! Run upstairs! I'll protect you!"

He was distressed that at this dangerous hour his parents were not here to help. But they never were home; they were always at the store, giving up their lives to business, ignoring the threats to their children's safety and well-being.

Only Kafka saw the thing. What could he do? He was not strong enough to destroy, or even defy, the deafening machine. All he could do was alert his sisters. He looked around for a weapon to defend them with. There was nothing in the house but a kitchen knife.

The machine stopped in front of the apartment house. While its engine continued to run, the operator stepped down to the street. He was carrying a package and some letters. On the side of the package, there was a large black *H*, and under it there was an equally large black *K*.

Franz felt a pleasant sensation. He knew the letters must be for him because he had been waiting impatiently for certain letters to arrive. He had become sad and anxious over the delay. When he came home from work and they hadn't come, he was disappointed, ate his tasteless dinner alone and went straight to bed, trying to sleep away his anxiety and regret. And that was where he was when he discovered that his sisters were threatened and he heard the ominous rumble of the machine.

He put on his clothes and went to the door. His sisters still had not come in and he began to worry. Then the doorbell rang. He looked through the window panel and saw the face of the driver of the machine. It was no longer an expressionless face; it transmitted contradictory feelings. On the one hand, the blue eyes were cold and penetrating. On the other hand, they also seemed to suggest a great inner suffering, a kind of martyrdom. They were the eyes of an angry victim.

Franz was baffled. Should he open the door? Where were his sisters? Why weren't they heeding his call? He desperately wanted those letters, although he had no idea what the package was.

Finally, he opened the door, but the package and the letters were no longer in the hands of the machine driver. He was gone. They were now carried by his giggling sisters who passed him by irreverently, without even giving him the mail he longed to receive.

He looked out into the street.

"Where is the machine?"

"What machine?" Ottla asked, laughing.

"The one that was going to run you over. The one you were screaming about. And where is the driver? He was right here a second ago."

His sisters weren't even listening to him.

He sat down to open his mail, but the letters he was waiting for were not there. And the package was addressed to Hermann Kafka, his father.

Chapter Two

As he walked home from work, Kafka brooded over his great embarrassment. What a fool he was! What a guilty fool! The whole mess was uncontrollable; he had absolutely no idea that it could happen, and yet it did.

He and Karl Blau had asked to see the President of the company, The Workers' Accident Insurance Institute, in order to express their thanks for being promoted. It was a very special meeting and they dressed for it in formal black suits. After all, Dr. Otto Pribram's position was so exalted, they might as well be having an audience with the Emperor.

Stepping a pace forward, Karl gave the President a little speech of gratitude that he and Franz had composed. While Franz was listening to it, he was struck by the ridiculousness of the situation. There the President sat, in a terribly dignified but somehow funny pose, his head lowered as if he were receiving a secret message, his white beard spread out over his chest like a throw rug.

Two grown men, responsible employees, strove humbly before him like swine before a God. Suddenly, Franz was attacked by a fit of giggles that he could not control. At first, he tried to conceal it by putting his hand to his mouth and coughing lightly. Everybody knew he was not well and that it was perfectly normal for him to have some respiratory discomfort. But when Karl finished and stepped back into place next to Franz and Dr. Pribram began speaking, he cast all of his pompous self-importance into a speech about the accomplishments of the Workers' Accident Insurance Institute as a direct result of the diligence and loyalty of its employees. Under the pressure

4

of this nonsense, Franz lost control of himself altogether, even while, under great stress, he continued to try to conceal his laughter.

Struck by a Presidential remark, Karl began to comment on one of his superior's ideas. He held forth at some length to a man who was totally indifferent to other people's opinions. This irony only made Franz laugh the louder since, he was really shaking with fear at his and Karl's offensive behavior. Excuses were hastily made, Dr. Pribram accepted them without delay, since it was impossible for him to imagine that anyone could think he was a ridiculous old man.

Hastily dismissed, Karl and Franz staggered out into the hall, roaring with laughter. But Franz was deeply ashamed and miserable about the debacle he had caused. Clearly, he'd have to write a detailed letter of apology and lay the blame for his wicked behavior at the door of his well-known physical ailments.

As he was trying to decide how to phrase this letter, he approached the cathedral and saw a street artist sketching on a large pad. As he got closer to the young man and saw his face, he realized that he looked like the machine driver in his dream, except that this young man was dressed shabbily and was altogether much more pathetic-looking. The man in his dreams may or may not have been dressed better, but that did not matter because the expression on his face made such considerations trivial.

Franz paused by the side of the artist and saw that the sketch was not only accurate in detail, but was a reasonably sophisticated rendering. He thought weakly of his own stick-figure sketches, which were no more than doodles, of tiny men fighting, running, crawling and kneeling on the ground.

"You've chosen a lovely day for your work," Franz said.

Quickly, the eyes of the young man alighted on him.

"Oh, yessir," he answered. "I've sure lucked out today."

Picking up the unfamiliar dialect, Franz asked him if he'd been in Prague long.

"Just pulled in from Vienna," the young man said. "I was told this city is an artist's dream, with castles and cathedrals and all. I decided to come and take a look-see for myself."

"And sell your pictures?"

"You bet. I've got a pretty thrivin' business goin' in Vienna but I ran out of buildings to copy. I work with a fellow who sells them for me. You an artist?"

"No, no" Franz said, too full of denial. "No, I… well, I do a little writing… from time to time."

"Do you?" the young man said. "That's one of my ambitions, too."

He scrutinized Franz's formal clothes.

"If you don't mind my saying so, you don't look it. What I mean is, you don't look like a writer."

Franz felt embarrassment again. Why was he always on the defensive, even with this threadbare…

"I have a job," he explained. "That's where I'm coming from now… I do my writing at night."

The young man returned to his sketching, but made it clear by an ever so slight tilt of his head in Franz's direction that he wished to continue the conversation.

"Tha'd be tough for me—working at night," he laughed.

Franz was charmed by the artist's ease. Here he was in a distant city, yet he appeared to be quite at home. At the moment, Franz felt himself to be a stranger and intruder.

"Where are you staying?" he asked.

The artist shrugged.

"Oh, I don't know. There must be a hostel around. When it gets dark, I'll look for one. Right now, I don't wanna waste the light."

"And you have enough buyers of your work to make a living?" Franz asked, studying the artist's face. He was already envious of the young man's self-confidence.

"I certainly do. I knock off the sketches, my partner sells them."

As Franz peered closer at the sketch, he got a whiff of uncleanliness. The young man's long hair was greasy and a stench boiled up from him when he moved. Franz backed away.

Because of his extreme revulsion against dirt, smells and disorder, Franz considered breaking off the conversation and going home to his dinner and his bed, but the young man's independence of spirit attracted him. Here was a young man—a struggling artist—who did not appear to submit to his insecurities, who took his risks and chances, and pursued his ambition. Look at himself now: a bureaucratic slave, burdened with a desk job in a large institution, a job that was actually making him sick.

And what was worse, he was surrendering to that institution his best and freshest hours each day and then was being forced by these miserable circumstances to find an hour or two in the middle of the night to drive himself crazy trying to do some decent writing. How much simpler things would be if he could turn all of his energy and skill to writing stories and making every effort to sell them! Take a risk! Take a chance the way this young man did who was sketching gaily in the bright afternoon. He had no idea of where he was going to sleep that night, what he was

7

going to eat, nor what he was going to encounter in a strange city. It didn't seem to matter.

This envy was only the second reason that Franz stayed. There was, primarily, the young man's similarity to the machine driver in his dream. It seemed peculiar that this pleasant and easy-going artist from Vienna could frighten his sweet sisters, but Franz could not put the intimation out of his thoughts. Convinced of the importance of his dreams for use in his stories, Franz decided to linger.

"Say," the young man said after he had finished off a corner of the cathedral, "if you're a writer, would you like to write a verse or two to go with the picture? Maybe it'll raise the value. If I sell copies of it, I'll give you some of the profits."

Franz was surprised at this forthright offer. The young man seemed natural and guileless, two characteristics he rarely found among his educated friends.

"I've… I've never written any poetry," Franz stumbled.

"What do you write?"

"Stories, sketches… mostly unfinished. They're not any good."

"You never know. Ever try to sell any of 'em?"

"Well, yes…"

"And…?"

"I got them published only because I've got friends with connections."

"That's wonderful!" the young man said. "That's just what I need—connections. Especially in Vienna. If I do a real nice watercolor of this cathedral, I could make room for a verse and put it right on the painting. Bet it would sell. Wanna try it?"

Franz was feeling uncomfortable. He knew that he had nothing to say about the cathedral that any tourist or watercolor buyer would be interested in.

"Thank you," he said, "but I don't think I'm the man for it."

The young man stilled his pencil and looked up at Franz candidly.

"I'll bet you're not a Jew," he said. "Are you? You're too laid back for a Jew."

His face turned hard and cold.

"Am I right?"

Shrinking inside himself, Franz said, "No."

The young man looked relieved. He pointed his pencil at Franz and said:

"There! I knew it! I just knew it! There's certain things you just know."

Even though Franz was disgusted by his remarks, the young man's arrogance had a bizarre appeal.

"Well, then," the artist went on, "you must know what I'm talkin' about. There must be plenty of Jews in Prague. Vienna's stuffed full'a them, I'll tell ya."

"Well, yes…" Franz said.

"So what do you say, Mr…?"

"Kafka."

"So what do you say, Mr. Kafka? My name's Alf, by the way. So what do you say? Wanna collaborate? You're the first person I've met in Prague; maybe you'll bring me luck… bring both of us luck because I can see you're not a happy man."

Franz shrank again. He thought he had succeeded in compartmentalizing his life and his feelings, and yet this hick, who was clearly not from Vienna—not originally, anyway—this itinerant street artist was able to see right through his disguise. Franz was anxious, but also curious.

"How do you know that?" Franz asked.

"I'm an expert in unhappiness," Alf said. "Seen too many people do what they have to do instead of what they want to do. I was like that until I left home."

He returned to his sketching.

But Franz wanted him to keep talking. The young man's openness and airy self-confidence were both refreshing and sweetly naive. He was certainly no success, judging from his appearance, but he didn't seem to be inhibited by his situation. Impoverished though he was, he was doing his art, he was out of doors instead of locked up in a gloomy office building doing work he was contemptuous of, and he traveled around to see and sketch Europe's wonderful sights-something Franz would be too cautious to do. That took courage.

How eager he had been to find a secure job after getting his law degree. Hadn't that been his main preoccupation and goal, even though the only thing he really wanted to do was write? He didn't care about the law, he didn't care about the job. All that concerned him was the security it would bring. Here now, right in front of him, was a young man, with much less education and training, who had already leaped across barriers which paralyzed Franz.

Should he write a verse or two for him? He couldn't possibly. Everything that mattered to Franz was invisible to the eye, including this cathedral that he knew so well and whose bells he awoke to every morning. Sketching and painting the surface of things could only be the preliminary step to understanding their complexities that were invisible to the naked eye. It seemed to him that sketching and painting could not possibly be the young man's final ambition.

"Have you been to art school?" Franz asked.

"I have, sir," Alf said. "Vienna has the best. You must have heard of the Art Academy. A tough school. I went there, and also took classes with Professor Gruber of Munich at his private school. I really want to be an architect. What I really want to do is build. I want to demolish the old buildings and create new ones."

Franz watched his head tilt upwards and his eyes reach skyward, beyond the cathedral's spires. They became fixed on some definite point Franz knew he himself wouldn't be able to see.

"I can show you some of the sights," Franz said, "and save you the time of hunting them up yourself."

"Thank you, Mr. Kafka," the young man said, "but I don't want to take up your valuable time. I'll be here just a few days and…"

"It's no bother. I can help you find a place to stay."

Franz thought about those two innocent sentences. Did he mean to intimate that, if he were going to stay longer in Prague, he'd be eager to take up his time? And why did this appealing hickish artist continue to remind him of the man in his dreams? It wasn't difficult to see behind his Viennese facade. Could he uncover it by some probing?

In a certain sense, this young man reminded him of Max Brod, an even more hopeful fellow who, after all, was still stuck with a crazy mother, a distant father, and a job he hated almost as much as Franz hated his.

"That's very kinda you, Mr. Kafka," Alf said, "but I've got to finish this."

"I'll tell you what," Franz said, "why don't you meet me at the Café Arco later on and we'll help you get set up for the night."

"We'll?"

"My friends and I."

"It won't be too much trouble for you?"

"No, not at all. After all, it's our city and you're our guest. Anyway, I want my friend Max to meet you."

"I'm much obliged," Alf said.

Franz took a pad and pen from his pocket and wrote down the directions to the Café Arco.

"Just ask anyone if you get lost," he said, handing him the piece of paper. "Everybody knows the Café Arco. It's a popular spot. I'll be there about six."

Chapter Three

As usual, no one was home. That's the way he liked it because he could perform his rituals without interruption. He could eat a little, do his exercises, take a nap, then prepare himself for the rigors of the Café Arco, which was a place he didn't find as congenial as Max did.

But first he'd better call Max at the post office. What would he tell him? That he'd just bumped into an itinerant Viennese painter of postcard art and they were going to treat him to dinner at the Café Arco? Max would be shocked. How many times had he tried to get Franz to come out for an evening, just for some society and conversation, and how many times had Franz said no? He loved Max, but among large numbers of people he got confused and couldn't concentrate. Max knew about his strange ways and he was trying to help Franz come out of his shell. But this? Yes, Max would be shocked.

Maybe he should start by telling him about his dreams—that would be more in character—then add the business about meeting the young man. What was his name? Alf. He would tell Max about this young man's clear-cut career decisions in favor of art, even though he was just an uneducated hack. And yet what counted more— the decision or the talent? He didn't know anymore.

Better yet, he'd simply leave a message. Please tell Dr. Brod to meet Dr. Kafka at the Café Arco at six o'clock this evening. Then he wouldn't have to do any explaining on the phone.

After the call, Franz stripped himself naked, opened all the windows and performed his exercises. Calisthenics were one of his few means to good health and he was sure he could see some improvement in his thin frame.

In his bathrobe, he ate his dinner of yogurt, nuts, and fruit, making sure that he chewed his food dozens of times before swallowing it.

Satisfied that he was doing his best to protect his inadequate body against early ruin, he lay down for a nap. It had been a particularly crazy day—and night, considering his dream—and the problem of falling asleep for an hour was far more difficult than it was on other days. But if he were going to stay up and write all night (or try to write), he'd have to get some sleep now. And yet, hammering at his consciousness were three or four burdens that would not diminish no matter what he tried to do about them. All he could do was doze off, a restless troubled doze that left him weak in the joints when he got up, and empty in the head. He couldn't think straight for the hour it took him to clean up, dress, and walk to the Café Arco.

Max squinted through his glasses when he first saw Franz. They had arrived at the Café Arco at the same time, and they stood outside exchanging amenities and relieving Max's anxieties. They were an amusing pair to look at from a distance, especially if the distance were being traversed by the eyes of a young postcard artist who had concealed himself in a doorway while waiting for his meal ticket to show up.

The Kafka fellow was tall and thin with ears that were so big, he looked like he might fly away. If not fly away, then follow a casket down the street because he looked as morose as any undertaker.

The other fellow was small and deformed, something close to a midget with an enormous head. Ugly people, these Czechs. Maybe not as filthy as the Viennese, though.

"Meet you at the Arco?" Max was saying. "I couldn't believe my ears. Are you all right? Are you finally taking my advice?"

"Not really," Franz said with a guilty smile. "A couple of things happened today and I want your advice. Let's go inside. There's not much time because someone is coming."

"Who?" Max asked, squinting again.

To further the absolute contrast between him and Franz, Max was blond and fair-skinned. All of these contrasting external features were indications of the temperamental differences between the two friends. As hard a life as Max had experienced, it did not seem to influence his sunny disposition, his hopefulness, his bursting optimism. Yes, he had to put up with the boring routine of his administrative job at the post office, but that only seemed to fire up his literary energies. As for his dark friend, everything put a damper on his delicate talents—his parents, his health, his living conditions, his job. But Max knew talent when he saw it, and if he had to be a spiritual and literary nurse to this gloomy patient, that's exactly what he would do, and that's why he rushed to meet Franz promptly at five.

They took seats at a booth in the dark coffee house. Max ordered coffee and Franz a glass of celery water.

"This has been an Alice-in-Wonderland day for me, Max," Franz began, "and you've got to help me sort it out. Lewis Carroll said that he placed a white stone next to the dates of important events in his life. Well, this was one of those days for me. Meanwhile, this fellow is coming…"

"What fellow?" Max asked.

He had a large nose protruding from his very large head, and when he got inquisitive, Franz thought it got even larger.

Franz bent over the table and, in a guarded way, outlined the day's events and then backtracked to his dream of the night before.

"Have you put any of this in your journal?" Max asked.

This question was typical of Max. He was constantly encouraging, provoking, even begging Franz to write things down.

"I haven't had time to," Franz said with a shake of his head. "My question is should I write a letter to Dr. Pribram and what should I say in it? How should I come off? How much should I confess? After all, he's the man who got me my job in the first place. If it wasn't for knowing his son…"

"A letter's no problem," Max said.

"Then, with all this spinning in my head, I went ahead and struck up a conversation with a street artist from Vienna and I ended up inviting him to meet us here. I told him that I'd show him some of the city's sights…"

"A big step forward," Max said. "That's very nice. You're getting sociable. I can see all my efforts are beginning to pay off."

"You don't understand," Franz said. "Don't forget the dream."

"The fact that he looked like the man in your dream?"

"Yes. I find that very upsetting."

Max reached across the table and patted his friend's arm.

"It was only a dream. I'd be more concerned about your writing, and laughing in front of Pribram. How could you do such a thing?"

"I don't know," Franz said. "I had no control over it. In a way, it was like a dream, but dreams often make more sense because they're always about our day-to-day experiences, no matter how distorted."

"The difference is if it was a dream, you wouldn't have to write a letter," Max said adding wittily, "except in another dream."

"I want to get to the bottom of that dream. My sisters were threatened. Why couldn't it have been my father? I'd have forgotten about it already."

"You're overreacting," Max said, sipping his coffee. "It's just a coincidence that the man in your last night's dream looks like the man you met today. What are you trying to say? That a schlemiel of a postcard artist is going to threaten your sisters, whom he doesn't even know? You're getting more sociable, if you don't let your paranoia get out of hand. Now all I've got to do is find a nice permanent girlfriend for you…"

Franz's gray eyes refocused and looked behind Max.

"He just walked in. Here he comes."

"Relax," Max said.

Franz got up and motioned to the young man, who had his sketch pad with him.

"Did you have any trouble finding it?" he asked as he reached the table. "Were my instructions clear enough?"

"Yes, and I got a real good look at your city. I'm glad I came."

"Did you find any good subjects?" Franz asked, but without waiting for an answer introduced him to Max.

"Max, this is the artist I told you about. Alf…"

"Adolf, really," the young man said. "Hitler."

"Hitler," Max said. "There are some Hitlers in Prague."

"Maybe," Alf said. "Used to be Hiedler, all kinds of spellings. But it's Hitler now."

"I was telling…" Franz began, then realized he hadn't introduced Max.

"Excuse me, this is my friend Max Brod. He's a successful writer."

Alf and Max shook hands.

"It seems that just by luck, I've met the right people in Prague," Alf said. "I got off the train not knowing a soul, and then I met Mr. Kakfa and…"

"Dr. Kafka," Max said.

"Oh?" Alf said, startled and impressed. "Dr. Kafka, sir… and we just started talkin'."

"Alf has an interesting philosophy of life and art, Max," Franz said.

"I do?" Alf said.

"Yes," Franz said. "He says you can't separate the two."

"Oh," Alf said, not having thought of philosophy in this regard. "Well, I guess you can, but I won't."

Franz looked piercingly at Max, as if to say, "There, didn't I tell you?"

"Everybody in my family was trying to discourage me," Alf said, "even my teachers. Go the easy route, they said. Do what we did; become an official."

"Your father, too?" Franz said.

"Especially my father," Alf said. "The old gentleman and I didn't see eye to eye on many things including my career. But it all worked out."

"How?" Max asked.

"He died."

The bluntness of the response made Max and Franz laugh.

"He was much older than my mother... And then my mother died, and so there was no reason to stay around, so I left home."

"Suppose your parents were still alive?" Franz asked.

"I'd have done what I wanted anyway. My mother was always on my side; it was my father who disapproved. The old gentleman used to get very angry at me."

"We've known parents like that," Max said.

"So are you fellas sayin' you can separate the two?" Alf asked.

"Not that we want to, but we do," Max said.

Looking directly into Franz's eyes, Alf said, "Scared of takin' chances?"

The hard gaze made Franz feel uncomfortable.

"Listen," he said, "you must be hungry. Why don't you order a meal? I've eaten already..."

"So have I," Max said.

"Go ahead and order," Franz said, handing him a menu.

"I can't say I don't have an appetite," Alf said, "but how much does it cost?"

"Don't worry," Franz said. "It's on us."

"And you're not having anything?"

"I'll have another coffee," Max said.

"Celery water," Franz said.

"I'm gonna dig in," Alf said, "'cause I got a big appetite, almost as big as my appetite for painting. As soon as I scrape together a little more money, I'm gonna wander through Italy sketchin' the whole country, and put together enough material for a year. Ever been to Italy?"

"Just the north—for a few days," Max said.

"Their sense of harmonious proportion is what I want to see. They were the greatest painters from the fifteenth to the seventeenth century. But today their art is degenerate."

19

"Why so?" Max asked.

"Because they don't see the connection between art and life. Art should be for the people."

"I HEARD THAT," a voice shouted, coming in for an attack. It was blind Oskar Baum, directing his strong but wary body at the voices. "What's this I hear? Folkish propaganda in the Café Arco?"

"Oskar!" Max Brod said, getting up. "Sit. Sit here. Can you see where you're going?"

"More than anyone thinks," Oskar said with a laugh. He was walled-eyed and had the permanent squint of the impaired. His high white forehead and thin eyebrows only served to dramatize his condition.

"We have a guest this evening," Max said, making room for him.

"So I just heard," Oskar said. "Folkish art. Who is this voice from the past? No, I mean, from the dead!"

Franz did not like Oskar's rowdiness and impertinence, especially now that he came on so intimidatingly. Would he drive the young man into silence?

"We have here a young artiste from Vienna," Max said with the slightest touch of ridicule in his voice. "Franz ran into him at the cathedral. Now treat him nicely. He's our guest."

Assuming Alf was uncomfortable at this invasion, Max tried to explain Oskar. But he was also doing it for Franz in the hope of relaxing him and allaying the claustrophobic pressure he felt whenever contentious voices were raised.

"This is Oskar Baum; he's another writer."

"I wouldn't put it that way," Oskar said. "Another writer?"

"What I meant to say," Max continued, "before I was so rudely interrupted, is that this place is a sort of literary hangout for…"

"…and Oskar Baum has the honor of being the blind bard of the group," Oskar said, "thanks to a street brawl between Czech patriots and German sausage eaters. As a result, I am very loud, radical, and unforgiving."

"As a result?" Max scoffed. "I never knew you any other way!"

"I'm an anarchist one day, a socialist the next—anything but a member of the status quo. So when I hear the words folk art, I reach for a brick!"

Franz wanted to jump up and run out the door. This is just the situation he wished to avoid. It was why he never came to the Arco. He couldn't stand people like Oskar Baum who used his handicap as a weapon. He also knew that Oskar was having a terrible effect on Alf. He could see the street artist retreating.

"Hello, Franz," Oskar said, turning his guns on a man he considered beyond help. "Slumming tonight?"

"No," Max said, "we're just trying to get a meal for our friend here."

"Well, how do you do, folkish friend," Oskar said, thrusting his hands over the table.

Alf rose part of the way, extending his hand which then clasped Oskar's searching one.

"May I join this conversation," Oskar said, "or is it too heady for my intelligence?"

"No sir," Alf said.

"But first," Max said, "let's get Hugo over here so we can order his meal."

When Oskar's voice thundered through the café, Hugo appeared and took the order.

21

The Arco was filling up with patrons and it was noisy. Food, drink, and tobacco were minor accompaniment to the strenuous vocalizing that came from every booth and table. Franz felt trapped. He was nearly in a panic caused, finally, by Oskar's unwanted and irritating appearance. In a state of confusion, Franz could not focus his attention on any one person or any one comment. He was the audience for the noise that encircled him. If anyone were to ask him a question, his answer would be incoherent. Oskar, almost totally blind, aggressive Oskar—particularly appealing to the ladies, Max had told him—was always at the center of debates. Any debate, Max said, for he had opinions about everything.

"Our guest here," Max explained to Oskar, "was saying that there cannot be a separation between art and life, as, for example, most of us represent, stuffed into the bureaucracy everyday and raging against it in our writing at night."

"And what does Mr...?"

"Hitler..."

"Mr. Hitler, who hasn't got a drink..."

"Beer."

"Hugo! What the hell is the matter with him? Why don't they hire a few more waiters? Beer, here. Two. Franz, are you...?"

"Celery water."

"Ah, yes," Oskar said with mild contempt. "And what does Mr. Hitler do to avoid the disgusting bifurcation in our lives?"

Alf paused in order to digest the word 'bifurcation.'

"I'm a painter and I want to be an architect."

"Really? And what do you paint, may I ask?"

"I've a little business in Vienna painting famous buildings."

Oskar's one barely usable eye searched Max and Franz.

"And?"

"I sell 'em."

"And this is how you mesh art and life?"

"I don't work for anyone," Alf added. "I never have. And I never will. Someday I'll be an architect and you'll visit my buildings."

"Can I see a sample of your work?"

"I just have the sketch of the cathedral I was workin' on this afternoon."

"Let's see it."

Franz shut his eyes. He knew what was coming and he didn't like it. He berated himself for not anticipating this. They should have gone to a less popular restaurant where he could have studied the young man of the dream without interruption.

Alf reached down and brought the sketch pad to the table top. He opened it and held up the sketch for everyone to examine.

"Oh," Oskar breathed sardonically," I see."

He aimed his usable eye at the sketch, then at the street artist.

"I see. I see you haven't heard of the twentieth century."

"Sir," Alf said with a note of surprise.

"Isn't your work somewhat literal? Haven't you seen the Impressionists, the Futurists? Van Gogh? Kokoschka? The Expressionists?"

"I have," Alf said, "and don't like them. They're degenerate. What can be in their minds? They hate nature."

"It's what they see," Oskar said. Franz could see he was readying his verbal hammers.

"Then they're blind," Alf said. "They have no hearts. They have no vision. They have nothing to say. They give the people nothing."

He fired off these sentences in a new way and Franz's heart gave a kick as he caught a glimpse of the man in his dream. The young man's reserve was falling away and being replaced by an unexpected forcefulness. Franz was looking out his window again and seeing the malignant expression on the face of the man in the machine.

"I have studied them, sir," Alf continued, "and they are without any spiritual values. You ask me about the separation of art and life. What is the result? Modern art! An art that totally lacks values. An art that has no center."

Oskar, with folded arms, listened to Alf. There was a sneer on his face.

"What book of clichés have you been reading?" he said. "I shouldn't be surprised. Your ideas are like your sketch."

I know that sneer," Alf said, stiffening. "I've seen it a thousand times in Vienna. I've seen it among you bureaucrats as you squat in your cages. That sneer is the essence of the modern, of your socialist and anarchist thought."

What's happened to his accent? Franz thought. It had suddenly disappeared. The hick was gone.

"And what do you want to replace it with?" Oskar retaliated. "Your folk art and folk culture? Your tribal myths? Your world of fake heroes known as the New German Man?"

Oskar turned to Max.

"Tell him, Max. Tell this Teutonic throwback a thing or two."

24

"Oskar," Max pleaded, "leave him alone; he's our guest."

"I came here in peace," Alf said. "I did not come for an argument."

He shot a frigid glance at Franz which froze him.

Hugo appeared with a tray of steaming food.

"No hard feelings, Alf," Max said. "This is the coffee house atmosphere. We go at each other like this all the time."

He pointed a finger at almost blind Baum.

"And Oskar leads the attack."

"Who gets the dinner?" Hugo asked.

The smell of food caused a wave of nausea to pass through Franz's stomach. Now he had to watch someone eat! Why had he lowered his guard and stuck himself in this pig pen?

"He does," Franz said, pointing at Alf while driving his body away from the food.

"I don't want any," Alf said, waving the food off. "I want to know how you expect to create vision in a people with art that's degenerate? What does it give? What does it offer? Nothing."

"It's a reflection of the way things are, of the way we live!" Oskar said.

"Who gets the dinner, then?" Hugo said impatiently.

"Not me," Alf said.

Franz waved it away with a panicky shake of his hand.

"I'm taking it back," Hugo roared, "but you ordered it."

"Take it back, take it back," Franz said, nearly sick to his stomach. "We'll pay for it."

"That's a pathetically weak answer," Alf said to Oskar. "Your art has made people rootless. You have stolen their dreams. You are cut off from the sources of inspiration."

Alf broke off and looked at the receding figure of Hugo and the free dinner he had lost. Franz saw his hunger but he knew that the man would never reveal how needy he was. Not now.

"Give it to someone else," Max shouted to Hugo.

"But it's on your bill!" Hugo shouted back.

"What are these primitive words you are using?" Oskar shouted at Alf. "Where do you get them from? How deep in the backwoods are you? Inspiration, dreams, heart, the people. You're in the wrong century, my friend. Wagner's been dead thirty years—thank God!"

Max's prohibiting hand shot up.

"Not Wagner again, Oskar! We dragged him over the coals last week."

Oskar sneered, seeing recognition on the street artist's face.

"Of course," he said, "you're a Wagnerian, aren't you? You cry at his operas, you weep at his myths and tunes, you long to run around the wilderness in search of the ring, or the grail, or the spear. You want to play in the woods like Karl May's Indians."

"I am not a Wagnerian," Alf sputtered. "I am a German, and after living in that cesspool of Vienna long enough, I know what that means. I believe in the spirit of Faust which says, 'You have destroyed it, the beautiful world; build it again, in your breast rebuild it.'"

They watched Alf take his fist and draw it to his chest, pressing it there, digging at the breastbone.

"There go the buzz words," Oskar went on, relentlessly. "Can't you utter a sentence without using them? There isn't an enlightened person today who takes Wagner seriously."

"Not in a place like this," Alf stormed. "Not among these…"

"These what? Europe is full of these places," Oskar interrupted. "You'll see that if you visit cities instead of forests."

"I meant to say," Alf said undaunted, "houses of ill repute, filled with Bolshevik thought."

"Ho! You'll have trouble finding a Bolshie around here."

Oskar swung his arm around the café.

"Everyone of these guys has a bourgeois father."

"And maybe no mother!" Alf taunted. "If they had mothers, they wouldn't be so remote from the people, so selfishly cut off from the community."

Oskar swiveled his head and screamed towards the bar:

"More beer, Hugo, we're beginning to roll!"

When Oskar turned back to his antagonist, he met a stop sign. Alf's hand was outstretched, palm forward, like a policeman's.

"Sir, I didn't come to your beautiful city to argue with you, or anyone else. May we get on as friends?"

His calm had returned and so, Franz noted, had his accent. But Oskar would not retreat.

"We can't stop now," he pleaded. "I haven't been called a Jew virus yet, or a parasite in the body of the people. That's how I got this," he said, pointing to his completely shut eye, "right after being called a Christ-killer and the lowest form of organic life by six pure German youths."

They all waited to see if Alf would take the bait. Franz knew there was a moment—a moment he had witnessed in his dream and would never forget—when the young man would put an end to all reserve and strike out at his enemies. Franz had felt driven to that point with his father

27

many times and only his superhuman self-control kept him calm.

For Alf, the moment came, and passed, in silence.

Hugo came with four more beers and splashed them down in front of the men, forgetting that Max and Franz were drinking coffee and celery water. The odor of the beer made Franz gag, so he inched it across the table toward Alf.

"As I recall," Alf said, "we were talkin' about art and life and how to keep yourself pure in the pursuit of…"

"Another buzz word," Oskar shouted. "Purity, oh, yes—racial purity, the mythic hero, the Parsifal in pursuit of pseudo-religious redemption…"

"Give the man a chance," Max said while relishing his friend's assault.

With deliberation, Oskar asked, "Why?"

"Because he's my guest," Franz said calmly.

"In that case," Oskar said, waving his hand submissively, "rave on."

"The main trouble," Alf said, "is that there is no deepness."

Oskar bowed his head and sniggered.

"Our lives are in pieces and there's nothing to hold us together. There is no set of values to live by."

Oskar drank noisily.

"When I first came to Vienna, I lived under the spell of the Ringstrasse."

"Spell," Oskar murmured.

"Yessir. It was an enchantment for me. I stood in front of the Opera and the Parliament for hours. The whole Ring Boulevard was somethin' stupendous to me. I'd never seen anything like it in my life, coming from a small town and livin' on the wrong side of the tracks in Vienna. But then I read a book in the library called *City Building* and I began

28

to realize that the beauty of the Ringstrasse was an empty one."

"Why?" Max asked.

"Because of the profit motive. I'll quote you from the author: 'All genius is tortured to death, all joyful sense suffocated—that is the mark of our time.' And then I saw the Ringstrasse as a front for decadent liberalism. I went into those buildings, I saw what goes on in Parliament. It was chaos. The city must be a true work of art, a total work of art in the service of a nation and its people. When art and life are separated, each corrupts the other. You gentlemen sound truly divided—one half of you locked in an office building, and the other half bitterly writin' about it at night."

Oskar finished his beer and got up.

"*Pardonnez moi*, but I have to eliminate. The beer, or something else, is filling me up too fast."

He took his cane and tapped his way toward relief.

"Are you coming back?" Max called out.

Oskar turned around.

"*Certainement*! Any enemy of the Ringstrasse's got to be a friend of mine."

Franz was glad to be rid of Oskar.

"Go on," he said to Alf. "I'd like to hear more."

"He's retreating," Alf said with a tepid smile.

"Not at all," Max said. "Oskar has trouble holding his beer."

Feeling his triumph, Alf said, "A coffee house regular has to do better than that."

"Go on," Max said. "Let's hear what you have to say."

"Well, I've talked too much," Alf said, "but these are my honest feelings. Modern art is diseased. It spreads dirt and decay; it makes us disgusted with ourselves. Is that what we want to pass on to our children? What happened to the tradition of Schiller and Goethe and Shakespeare?"

Max winked at Franz, then pointed to him.

"You've got to read one of his pieces," he said to Alf.

"No! Oh, no!" Franz erupted.

"I understand Dr. Kafka is a writer," Alf said. "He's very modest about it."

"You're sitting before a genius, sir," Max said. "His work is going to be read long after you and I... and Oskar...are forgotten."

"I believe you, sir," Alf said, "I truly do. I'd be honored to read a piece of your work."

"You haven't had your meal," Franz said. "Please order something."

"No, thank you, sir. I often find that discussion is food enough for me."

When Oskar didn't return, Franz suggested that they make sure Alf got a room at the Men's Hostel for the night.

"Tomorrow, I'll show you the sights. You'll have plenty of sketching to keep you busy. The hostel's in the old part of the city—where I live. It's very picturesque."

"After the slums of Vienna," Alf said with a courtly bow of his head, "I'm sure it'll be an improvement. Thank you, sir."

Chapter Four

Franz couldn't sleep. His mind was alarmingly alert. That was the price of showing up at the Café Arco. On top of that, this Hitler fellow, and on top of that, the dream. And then that stupid business at work with Dr. Pribram. And Oskar! He was an embarrassment. Why did he walk away? Was he vanquished? It almost seemed that way. He baited Hitler, but it was the visitor who knew when to stop, showing himself to be a lot shrewder than his Austrian manner suggested.

And yet Oskar had drawn Hitler out enough for Franz to see a trace of the potential harm he could do. Hadn't he? He saw the poison. Ah, his sisters. Why couldn't he have dreamed of his father in danger. Let the man on the machine come for his father. Oh, what a fight there would be. The victor would be in doubt, machine or not, but Franz wouldn't care one way or the other. That was the difference. Hermann Kafka could take care of himself, as all the Kafkas before him had. Why, Hermann's father could pick up a sack of potatoes with his teeth! How many times had he heard that one, to which he always sought a reply but could never think of one, and if he did he would always keep it to himself.

No, his father didn't enter his dreams or his nightmares, but his sisters did, regularly, and especially Ottla.

He resented any time he spent in the coffee houses. He resented talking, he resented argument, he resented discourse. Speech robbed everything of its seriousness and importance. There were too many subtleties that could not be expressed, and, as a result, there were too many falsifications and invalidations. There was too much of the saying of things for effect and not for the meaning which lay buried beneath other obvious meanings. For instance, Oskar's story about being blinded in the street brawl. The fact is that he was born blind in one eye and was eleven when he injured his other eye in a street brawl. In his argument with Hitler, he turned the brawl into an ideological battle. How do you fit the truth into the fevered atmosphere of a coffee house dispute?

This Hitler had his ways. He held himself back in the debate, but Franz could see the fury coming. His voice and accent were chameleon-like, and the young down-and-out artist seemed to be pretty well-informed. Why did Oskar leave? Was he merely responding to a call of nature? He would never know. If he asked him, he would invent something, puff up the truth. He would certainly not expose himself. If Oskar kept a diary, he might tell the truth there. Speech. To speak is to lie. No wonder he had become hysterical in Pribram's office. His laughter was in rebellion against the lie of speech, which he didn't have the courage to condemn outright, so his unconscious took over and threw him out of control.

But Oskar was right, too; Hitler's mind was limited and banal. He had done some reading, but what he read was re-routed among his banalities and drowned in a sea of clichés and buzzwords, as Oskar called them, and prejudices and absolutes. He had conviction all right, but it was the conviction of a mind that cannot grasp that words are not things and that concepts are fictions, and that God is an artifact of a particular language, a shadow thrown by grammar rather than a reality independent of it.

These thoughts irritated Franz's brain. He worked so hard at being solemn and unmovable, but today had been a day of serious errors and miscalculations. He had let go and been let go of, and now there were consequences.

Sleep was not coming, and now through the thin walls of his room he could hear his father huffing, puffing, and grousing while playing cards with his mother. He could even hear the angry slap of the cards on the table. If he got up and went inside, the war would continue.

What a mistake it was to go into business with him! Circumstances had looked promising and the idea of quitting his job and living off the factory profits was an insidious lure. That would give him the freedom to write and the freedom to get out of Prague whenever he wanted to. Those appealing lures totally sabotaged his judgment. He didn't know that he would end up with two jobs—one at the insurance company and one at the Prague Asbestos Works. Now that this was the case, all bets were off, because he was not going to sacrifice his writing for anything. If his father didn't understand that, he'd have to bear the consequences.

"Pardon me, Herr Sohn," his father would address him if he went into the room; his voice would be thick with sarcasm, "but don't you think you ought to put in an appearance at your own factory? Do you think those so-called employees of yours are going to do any work without supervision?"

"I'm ill," Franz would say, "I'm not well, don't you understand? I can't stand around and breathe that poison in!"

"Someone's got to be there," Hermann Kafka would shout. "Your brother-in-law's on a business trip, I've got the store to look after, and you get off at two o'clock in the afternoon! So tell me, Mister Artiste, who should go?"

"We've got a foreman!" Franz would answer. "He knows more about the asbestos business than the three of us."

"He's not family," Hermann would shout again, pounding the table. The cards would shake and float. Julie Kafka would try to protect them from ending up on the floor. "One of us must be there at all times! How did I get into this? Why did I listen to you? I knew I couldn't trust you to follow through!"

"I never said I'd work there as long as I had my job at the insurance company!"

At such moments his father's face would redden; he'd begin gasping; then his mother would send out the warning:

"Franz, please, your father's heart."

He pulled the sheet over his face. Sleep. Sleep. If only he could sleep. He was not going to get up and walk into that lion's den. Asbestos! He didn't care if the whole city burned down. It was already petrified and lifeless, anyway. He'd like to go to Munich to work and study there. He didn't have anything in common with Jews and it would be an opportunity to develop his German studies. Maybe he'd take off with this Hitler fellow. He had the right idea. Do what your spirit called upon you to do. Do what you're compelled to do. Pursue your own dreams. He may look impoverished—his mind certainly was—but he was free, even if his immediate goal was only to make money painting postcards for tourists.

Why not? He saw himself travelling from city to city until he found the right place to settle down, and then his real life would begin, free of his father, free of the desk job, free of the asbestos business. Maybe he'd bring it up while showing Alf the city tomorrow. He had told him he'd meet him at the railroad station but first he would arrange for his room at the hostel. Hitler didn't like the thought of the place. He was afraid there would be too many Jews sleeping with him.

"I'm poor," he told Franz, "but I don't defecate in the street like Jews."

Franz sighed. He was depressed again and he didn't feel like writing, which always made matters worse. When he wrote, he managed to escape the unrest, to shut out the loathsome voices around him. Like Flaubert, his writing was a rock to which he could cling in order not to be drowned by the waves of the world. Now that he was stonily conscious, the waves were mounting. He re-thought and revisualized last night's dream and the more he thought about the dangers to his sisters, the more calculating and determined he got. There was Ottla, his baby sister, a fiery little imp who went up against the old man with an abandon that shocked Franz. She had to put up with Hermann at the store everyday. When he thought of that as his own fate, he began thinking of suicide. When Ottla flirted with goys, she made her mother hyperventilate. Maybe, like Hermann, she had a little bit of the killer instinct in her. It was good for survival; he wished he had some of it. But like all Jews, they turned it against each other because it was too dangerous to go the other way.

What a family! He knew that the healthiest thing that could happen to them all was to split up, instead of living on top of one another. Ottla really had the right idea. She needed room, she was making her plans. Much to everybody's dismay, she had joined the Zionist Jewish Girl's and Women's Club and was attending meetings and lectures. She was even thinking about becoming a pioneer in Palestine, a member of a kibbutz.

Once again, he saw her cowering in the doorway of the butcher shop, hiding behind Elli and Valli. Ottla cowering? Ottla hiding? The image made him shiver. The danger must be greater than he first thought. He needed to be less calculating, less evasive. He needed, somehow, to spring a trap.

Chapter Five

He was late as usual. On his day off, he could keep his friends waiting for hours.

Hitler was outside the hostelry, having waited with patience. It was a beautiful day, the sky was clear, the blue of it sparkled. To Franz's eyes, Prague looked about as good as she could—" The little mother with claws," he had written somewhere. That about said it all. The natural thing to do was to escape the claws.

"Have you had breakfast?" Franz asked upon approaching the threadbare artist.

"Yes, yes," Hitler said. "Very adequate."

"I owe you a meal, you know," Franz said.

"How is that?"

"Last evening. There was so much turmoil. Oskar made such an ass of himself. I can understand why you refused to eat."

"You do?"

"Yes," Franz said. "I've done it myself. You refused to give into a simple human need."

He could see by the look on Hitler's face that he had taken him by surprise. In the fragment of time that followed, Franz imagined that Hitler was trying to decide how much of himself to reveal, but he made the mistake of moving on.

"I hope you have good strong shoes," Franz said, "because Prague..."

Hitler grabbed his arm as Franz was about to move.

"Why, if you're not a Jew, do you mingle with 'em?"

"Friends are friends," Franz said without a pause to reveal surprise at Hitler's bluntness. He was put completely off his guard and wanted to change the subject.

"Come on, now, I'm anxious to show you the city. Maybe this tour will improve my relationship with it."

"Maybe we're in the same boat," Hitler said.

"I don't know," Franz said. "Are you empty, detached, and lost?"

Hitler pulled his sketch book closer in order to use it as part of his answer.

"I'm looking for a subject."

Franz was surprised at the frankness of his remark about Jews, but now he felt he was withdrawing into ambiguity. Franz held out his arm, as if he were opening the door to the city.

"Let's go then," he said.

As they made their way across the Charles Bridge, Franz pointed out the location of every picturesque monument that this side of the city had to offer—churches, palaces, the Jan Huss Memorial, the National Theater. Hitler made quick notes so that he would be able to find the places on his own in days to come.

Trying to stay on the surface of things because he was afraid of Hitler's opening question, Franz pointed out, without comment, Wenceslas Square, the Old Town, the Jewish Quarter, and the street where he'd been born. But he slipped into a sardonic mode when they passed the Workers' Accident Insurance Institute on Poderbradstrasse. He called it "a precisely constructed machine of torture, the purpose of which is to prevent accidents."

He steered Hitler into alleys of the Old Town, past the German University where he couldn't avoid smelling the toilet reek that emanated from his venerable alma mater.

"It's all history and no comfort," he said of the cold damp rooms and halls. "But then, isn't that what history is—no comfort?"

He said that the many literary cafés—the coffee houses—were like catacombs where the remains of something long dead were examined.

As they crossed the Moldau River, he pointed out that, to innocents and tourists, it looked like the mighty Mississippi, but it was really only four feet deep at this point and was filled with leeches.

Prague was not what it seemed.

"Oh, yes, it's true that Mozart considered Prague his second home, but that was only because Figaro had been snubbed in Vienna."

By shitting a little in his own nest, Franz thought he might begin to break down Hitler's reserve to the point where, when he did open up, he would reveal even more than Franz had dreamed of.

When they stopped for lunch in the Kleinseite, at the hotel where Franz had recently brought a shopgirl for purposes other than eating, Hitler wanted to know why he had such contempt for his city.

"Why do you hate Vienna?" Franz countered.

"Because it makes me feel like a Jew," Hitler said.

"That's what Prague does to me, too," Franz said.

"But why should you feel like that? You have an important position. You are Herr Doktor Kafka."

"There's something secret and overpowering here that drains my energy. It's insidious."

"I know what you mean," Hitler said. "In the slums of Vienna, house after house is a brothel. While the youngest women make their money on bug-infested beds, their grandmothers sit outside and pick lice out of the children's heads. What they live in are more like cages than rooms, many families and tenants crammed together. In a room ten by fifteen, there'll be a dozen stinking people. Garbage covers the streets. Women perform their private functions in front of their houses, in full view of their neighbors. I thought I was gonna go mad there. I said to myself, 'This can't be: I, the son of Germans, living in a sewer!'"

"The Czechs say all the time that Jews and Germans have a lot in common."

"How can that be?" Hitler gasped, throwing his knife onto his plate.

He had been eating, with relish, a pork roast with dumplings and sauerkraut. Franz was disgusted by it and just picked at his vegetable omelet.

"We are part of the German Reich. We're not bound together with these sub-human nationalities. My God, the German is slipping, slipping..."

Franz had hit a target, and aimed again.

"The Czechs say the German and Jews both are outcasts. They're detested by everyone because they have no honor and no morals."

"That's vile," Hitler said. "To be thought of in the same breath. The German is being swallowed up by... by Croats, Serbians, Hungarians, Czechs, Jews and gypsies."

"Come on, finish your meal," Franz said sympathetically. He drank his celery water. "This subject really upsets you, doesn't it?"

Shaking his head and resuming his meal, Hitler said, "Yes, yes."

"The Jews predict all this in the story of the Golem," Franz said.

"The what?" Hitler said, his eyes fearful.

"You've never heard of the Golem? It's a Hebrew word that means a formless, mindless being, a verminous force. It happened here in the invisible Prague, the Prague of occult moods, the Prague you can't copy down on your sketch pad for tourists."

"Really?" Hitler said. "And what does this Golem do?"

Where was the threat to his sisters now? He stared at the gullible expression on a thin, papery face that was trying with little success to grow a moustache. Hitler's long pale hands with nails rimmed with Vienna dirt were clumsily grasping a knife and fork.

"You have to understand that this story is a creation of the Jews."

"You mean," Hitler said, "there's no real actual Golem?"

"One doesn't know for sure. That's where Jewish treachery comes in."

Hitler reached across the table and touched the sleeve of Franz's jacket.

"Dr. Kafka, sir, I want to say I am very pleased to have made your acquaintance. I would have been lost in this city... been ignorant..."

"Eat, eat," Franz said, "and I'll tell you the story. The Golem was created by Rabbi Loew in the sixteenth century. He had generative powers."

"You mean he created him like a Frankenstein?"

"Yes, only in reality. The creature was a man-like figure of clay who came alive when Rabbi Loew put a magic capsule called a *shem* into his mouth. At the beginning of the Sabbath, the *shem* had to be taken out of the Golem's mouth because the Golem must not be alive during the Sabbath. But one Friday evening, the Rabbi

41

forgot to remove the *shem* and the Golem went berserk and began slaughtering all the gentiles in Prague."

"My God! Why did he create the Golem in the first place?"

"Because the ghetto of Prague was being attacked, the women were being raped and the children roasted, and the Rabbi thought the end of the Jews had come, and so he created a miracle."

"A terrible destruction," Hitler said with the innocence and enjoyment of a child hearing a story from his father.

"A pogrom," Franz said. "When the head of the ghetto told the Rabbi to stop the slaughter, Rabbi Loew went to the Golem and quieted him down by singing him a song. He took the *shem* out of his mouth and the Golem ceased its slaughter."

"Temporarily," Hitler pointed out.

The expression on his face made Franz want to scream. He wanted to release a bolt of laughter into the coffee house. He wanted everyone to know what a gullible idiot the terrible man of his dream was. He had made up half the story; he might as well proceed with a few more creative touches.

"The Golem is Jewish revengefulness," Franz continued. "Today its eyes are closed, Rabbi Loew is long dead, and no one knows where the *shem* is. And he's right here in Prague."

"He is? Now?" Hitler asked. "The Golem?"

Franz had never studied Max's face as closely as he studied this man's. Even his own watery eyes and his own cadaverous face didn't get the scrutiny he gave this man.

"Yes." And pointing upward and outward, he said, "It lies in the attic of the Prague Synagogue. It's covered with centuries of dust and cobwebs."

42

"It's in this city?"

"Yes, and it may come alive again. I heard that the Jewish elders were asking if the Golem should be included in the congregation of worshippers since he is the oldest member of the synagogue."

"The *shem* must not be found," Hitler said.

"I think, with the rise of Zionism, it may come alive again."

"It might. I've heard of Zionism." Hitler bent over the table. "I must tell you—I rarely met a Jew until I came to Vienna. I knew one or two in Linz from a distance, and even then they made me panic. I couldn't breathe the air anymore. Did you ever feel that way? As if they had all the air to themselves? What was left for me?"

"I know what you mean," Franz said.

"Do you? I was very careful last night. Did you notice?"

"No."

"The way that Oskar fellow was goading me. He's a bad one. Maybe he has the *shem* and will bring it to the Golem."

"But Oskar is blind."

"He can be led there."

"By whom?"

"By his hatred for us. By those who will use their hatred to destroy Germans."

"There are many," Franz said.

"That's why Vienna was such a shock to me. I grew up in a small town of good loving people. The dedication of my mother…"

He pressed his hand to his chest.

"…will live with me forever."

"A true German mother," Franz said.

"God, yes." He had caught a sob and suppressed it. "She was clean, fair-minded and simple, and yet she was taken from me."

Franz masked his face with a compassionate expression.

"How?"

"A horrible disease. Of all people—this saintly woman. I'm not ashamed of my tears. I know you'll understand, Dr. Kafka. The worst thing about Vienna is the loneliness, not being able to tell anyone what you truly feel. I took care of my mother but I was helpless."

"Where was your father?"

Hitler waved that subject aside.

"He died many years before. No, it was me and my mother, and then the doctor. He butchered her and then she suffered even more through his treatments. She died in my arms and I've been alone ever since."

"Don't you have any brothers or sisters?'

"No. Just a humpbacked aunt who hates me."

"What happens now?"

Hitler shrugged, wiping his eyes.

"Now I paint and travel, dream and search."

"And your goal?"

"To go home in victory. To cure this wound I feel. What does Parsifal say: 'The wound! The wound! It burns within my heart!'"

Franz had had enough. If this barrage of sentimentality kept up, he'd plunge a knife into him. He knew who he was dealing with now.

"The quest for redemption," he said, looking deeply into Hitler's eyes.

"That's Wagner's greatest theme. He is the conscience of our time."

"Nietzsche called him the bad conscience."

"Who?"

"Nietzsche. The philosopher."

"He must be a Jew," Hitler said.

Watching his 'guest' enthuse over Hradcany Castle and St. Vitus' Cathedral, Franz wondered if he would survive these sentimental raptures and fuzzy-minded fantasies. A whole day of romanticizing was getting him sick and not any closer to the man of his dream. He had observed only the slightest glimpse of the man he was looking for, and all of those glimpses had occurred yesterday at the Café Arco. He was thinking about what to do next when he spotted Ottla as they were crossing the Franz Joseph Bridge.

She was not alone.

"Hello, Franz," she said cheerily and without a bit of self-consciousness at being caught with a German boy. "We're escaping to the park. Isn't it a beautiful day? This is Ernst Gerstl. Ernst, I'd like you to meet my brother, Dr. Franz Kafka."

As Ernst brought himself to his full height, bowed, and clicked his heels, Ottla's curious eyes were searching the face and figure of the young man with her brother.

"How do you do?" Franz said, wondering how Ottla was going to explain her behavior to their parents. "May I present Mr. Adolf Hitler of Vienna. He's an artist."

"An artist!" Ottla gushed. "How wonderful! Ernst is going to be an engineer."

"Sanitary," Ernst clarified.

"What do you paint?" Ottla asked.

"Buildings of historic interest," Hitler said. "I would like to be an architect."

45

"How ambitious!" Ottla said. "And here I am working all day in a dry goods shop. What does one have to do to become an architect?"

"Be able to plan," Hitler said. "To know what a city and a people need."

Here again, Franz heard Hitler altering his accent, upgrading his speech. He coughed in order to avoid snickering.

"My, my," she said, "what forthright answers."

"Well, ma'am, I've wanted to do it all my life."

"I was just telling Ernst that my ambition is to return to the soil. I hate the city," Ottla said.

Franz liked to observe his sister in the company of others. It revealed just how much she was growing up. Here she was, at nineteen, a center of attention, and a girl with a mind of her own. It was too bad that in her physical features she took after their bovine father's side of the family. Her mind, though, was as nimble as any Loewy's.

"My sentiments exactly," Hitler said. "I find the city exciting but uncongenial. I'm a country boy myself."

"Good," she said boldly. "Ernst will be needed in the city, and that's not for me."

"But I've got my career to pursue," Hitler said, "so it'll have to be the city for me."

"See," Ernst said to Ottla. "Listen to him. Why don't *you* understand?"

"Because you men have all the opportunities and we women get what's left over."

"Now, Ottla," Franz said, "do you have to have this argument on the bridge? It's bad enough in the house."

"The young lady has a point," Hitler said. "Women are strictly subordinated to men's wishes and careers."

"So," Ottla smiled, "a man who understands women. Finally!"

"Since they are the flowers of life, they must be cultivated."

Ernst Gerstl's eyes narrowed and he touched Ottla's hand.

"Come on, Ottla," he said.

Franz didn't like the look of it. He was sure they were heading for the lover's lane in the Kleinseite park. What if Hermann found out that this young man was not a Jew?

"Wait, Ernst," Ottla said. She turned back to Hitler and spotted his sketch pad. "How often do you meet an artist? Do you have any work I can see?"

"On this bridge, Ottla?" Franz said.

"Not yet," Hitler said. "Dr. Kafka has been showing me where everything is so I can make my own tour and start working."

"I'd like to go with you," Ottla said.

"Ottla!" Ernst said with a frown.

Franz was irritated, too. What made her so irrepressible? If he was the silent rebel in the family, she was more outspoken than all of her sisters and cousins combined. She had much of the force and energy that Hermann had used to reshape his life from Jewish peasant to successful German burgher.

"Excuse me," Ottla said. "Did I say something wrong?"

"My youngest sister gets a little rambunctious once in a while," Franz said to Hitler.

"I'd be honored to accompany you, mademoiselle," Hitler said.

Despite this appearance of Austrian warmth, a coldness passed through Franz and its message was: keep these two away from each other.

"Are you inviting Herr Hitler to our house for dinner, Franz?" Ottla said in retaliation.

"Oh, no thank you, ma'amselle," Hitler said.

"Oh, yes, yes," she insisted. "My father would *love* to meet an artist." She grasped her escort's arm. "Ernst is coming, too."

Franz wanted to laugh at his sister's impertinence. It was one of the reasons he loved her so much. She was a self-confident challenger who thought little of consequences. This aspect of her personality was beyond the range of possibilities for him, her decade-older brother with a law degree and an important position. No wonder Hermann had severe heartburn: he had, not one, but two extremists in the family. Well, it shouldn't be such a surprise. You can't be manic and not have it make an appearance in your children.

After Ottla said goodbye and walked gaily off with Ernst in the direction of lover's lane, Hitler stopped alongside Franz.

"Your sister is delightful and impetuous and I know she took you by surprise."

"Oh, no she didn't," Franz lied. "Living with Ottla, you learn to live with surprises."

"It wasn't quite fair of her to invite me like that," Hitler said.

"But now that she has, why don't you come for dinner and see what a German family is like in Prague."

"That's very kind of you, but I can't come like this. I've got… a nice shirt…" Hitler bowed his head. "Let me go back to the hostel. Just write down the directions and tell me what time to be there."

"We eat at six," Franz said, jotting down directions on the back of Hitler's sketch pad.

2

Chapter Six

First, of course, a little hysteria.

"Lenchen," Frau Kafka moaned to the cook, "do we have enough for two more at dinner?"

"I'll think about it," Lenchen said.

"What am I running? A hotel?" Herr Kafka sulked. "One day off and I get company. How about having a little consideration for your parents?"

"It's Ottla's fault," Franz said defensively. "She invited them."

"What's with that girl?" the head of the family complained. "She's always in my hair."

Lenchen said there was enough goulash for an army. Could she invite some of her relatives?

"Don't be impossible," Hermann Kafka snapped at her.

He did not like being overruled and bringing uninvited people to dinner on his day off overruled him. Now he wouldn't be able to belabor every problem through dinner and beyond. He wouldn't be able to drive Franz to his room or out of the house. If only he could get his son to eat out. And not only eat out! How about *move* out? Like Elli and Valli. Move out, get married. Normal things. Did Herr Sohn do anything normal? Watch him eat and you want to take the plate and throw it out the window—maybe with him attached to it! A vegetarian who made a normal dinner impossible because it wasn't enough for him to refuse meat, he had to make everyone at the table feel like a cannibal for eating flesh. It was too much to take from the only son!

"And when are you going to show up at the factory?" Herr Kafka shouted through the living room wall at Franz who had dropped the bomb and then retreated to his room. The retreat was hardly effective because the walls were paper thin and his room was stuffed between the living room and his parents'. Most of the time, he retreated only to suffocate.

Franz, lying on his bed, shut his eyes and set his mouth grimly.

"Next week!" he yelled.

"Next week?" Herr Kafka exploded.

"This week!" Franz corrected.

"And make it more than one day, Mr. Entrepreneur. It would be nice if your employees knew who you were!"

Franz threw his hands over his face. He had to get out of this house. He just had to! How was he going to write? How was he going to think? How was he going to eat right and exercise and keep his weight up? That factory was going to make his weak lungs weaker. What did his father care? It only mattered that the business do well, and then he'd complain how much better business could be! The man was obsessed, and nothing, nothing would ever change him.

Franz forced himself to think of the story he wanted to write about a young man who wanted to get away, to escape, but his tyrannical father condemns him to death by drowning. The young man obeys his father. Franz knew the ending, and the last line was already written. It was both powerful and subtle. Max said write it; he would have no trouble publishing it.

Pleased that he knew he would write it, he dozed off and dreamed that Ottla was at the window watching some young guy trying to get in. His mother and father were in the dining room playing cards. Ottla was smiling; the fellow was talking to her, saying he wanted to take her somewhere. He looked deformed. Was it Max?

Ernst Gerstl didn't show up. Ottla, the little manipulator, had probably found a way of sending Ernst home and making him think it was a good idea.

Hitler had washed up and found himself a suit. It wasn't much of a transformation, but he was more presentable, and, as far as Franz could tell, when he shook his hand, he didn't smell.

He even brought flowers. He groveled before Franz's parents, thickened his accent, and oozed Austrian charm. He said he was grateful for their hospitality four times in a half hour, and that it was Fate that had caused him to meet their son, the Herr Doktor, on the street.

"Most folks simply ignore me when I'm out sketchin'," he said. "I don't look like the most prosperous of men and yet your son engaged me in a most interesting conversation. He has made me determined to complete my education and be as well-informed as he is."

"That's the right attitude," Herr Kafka said. "You've got it. It's all a matter of hard work and keeping your nose to the grindstone. I don't know how you grew up, but we were poor, dirt poor. We were made of dirt. But I was a fighter. My father was a butcher and I had to deliver meat all over town in bare feet on winter days, and that's no exaggeration. Ask my family."

Ottla nodded mechanically. There was a slight play of mockery about her mouth.

"We were close, we were strong," Herr Kafka went on. "My father could pick up a sack of potatoes with his teeth. That's what the Kafka line is like."

"I know what you mean, sir," Hitler said. "I had the same kind of family. My father was a very strong man."

"What does he do?"

"He's passed on, now, but he was a customs official, a totally dedicated man, who, I might add, had the whole town's respect."

"Ah, that's important," Herr Kafka said. "Yes, yes, dedication. That's what I believe in, too. Nose to the grindstone. Dedication. But children today—I don't know. They've got it too easy. Don't you think so?"

"I certainly do. You're one hundred percent right, Herr Kafka. In my travels…"

"What do you do, by the way?"

"Well, I'm… plannin' to be an architect."

Herr Kafka's eyes widened.

"So!"

"I want to build. I want to make something useful that the whole community can be proud of. Right now, I'm in the learnin' phase, travelin' through cities to learn the tradition."

"Very good! Wonderful! My son, you know, is a lawyer. He has a very good position with the biggest insurance company in Prague. He's also in business with me."

"Oh, yessir," Hitler said, "I've already seen that he's a man of many talents."

Frau Kafka ate her soup. Franz and Ottla's eyes played on each other's sense of the ridiculous.

"True," Herr Kafka said. "Altogether, we're a thriving family."

"A tribute to German values," Hitler said.

"Most certainly."

"And I might add," Hitler said, turning to Ottla, "that you have a most charming daughter who I was privileged to meet this afternoon."

"Ottla, my baby," Herr Kafka said, patting her hand. "I don't know what my business would do without her. People come into the store just to chat with her."

"Do you find that you have much competition from the Jews? I know in Vienna…"

"Oh, we get along," Herr Kafka said. "The important thing is…"

"I was tellin' your son that it's hard for a young German without contacts to make his way. In my part of the city, the Jews own everything."

"Ah, here comes the goulash," Herr Kafka said with relief. "Right on time, Lenchen. We've just finished our soup. Hungarian goulash, Herr Hitler. Lenchen's masterpiece!"

Listening to all this perversion and bombast, Franz was near despair. Even the possibility of danger to his sisters did not fortify him against the banalities that passed between the guest and his father. And his always silent mother, listening to all of this, what was she thinking? It was a moment of spectacular relief when Hitler, a little drunk on German beer, and as a result more prolix than usual, felt it was time to leave. Another few minutes and Franz might have fallen asleep at the table. Not so these two true Germans who had found each other, or to be more precise had the luck to be introduced to one another by a Yid intellectual who would have preferred to be in his room reading Dickens or Dostoevsky.

What was a true son? A mirror. And here they were, perfectly reflecting each other's lies. One blowhard who was all ears for another blowhard's drafty mouth. They

53

were perfect company—Adolf Hitler and Hermann Kafka, sons of the soil and the people, rather than sterile urban intellectuals like Franz and his effete friends.

The parting was noisy and physical. They shook hands, his father pounded Hitler's thin back. He invited Hitler to visit his store in Kinsky Palace.

"You'll see a lot of architecture there," he told him proudly.

With the future architect out the door, Herr Kafka stared pitilessly at his only son while saying, "Now there's quite a young man. He's been around, he's a talker, he's got ideas and ambition. I'm happy you brought him here."

"I think he's cute," Ottla said.

Franz tried to terrify his sister with a sharp look.

"Well, I do!" she retaliated.

"The boy has ambitions; he's got dreams," Herr Kafka said. "I like him. And you know what else? He's grateful. He doesn't hold back his feelings."

There was no point in trying to contradict his father, so Franz left the room. He felt constricted, almost paralyzed. Ottla, that little… It was one thing to hear idiocies drop out of his father's mouth like spittle, but hearing Ottla get idiotic, too, was a great blow. Who was on his side? Why was he always alone in his opinions? In his cage of a room, still threatened by his father's obscene enthusiasms, he opened his journal and wrote:

> I think differently from the way I ought to think,
> I speak differently from what I think,
> I write differently from what I speak,
> and so it all proceeds into the deepest darkness.

Chapter Seven

That night Franz had another dream. He was a lot younger and he was standing in an open field watching Hitler build a castle and a ring of other buildings out of mud. He had created them quickly and he was very pleased with himself. Smiling, he showed them to Ottla who clapped her hands in joy and delight. Then, quite deliberately, Franz walked over and crushed the castle and other buildings with his feet. Large and forbidding, his father appeared and was enraged at what Franz had done. Wielding his fists about him, his father stomped on the ground, making it shake. Then he ran to Hitler to explain his son's behavior. He pointed damningly at the criminal who had done the damage. He embraced Hitler and the three of them—Hitler, Hermann Kafka and Ottla circled the ruins in a dance. Young Franz stood aside, observing, and only he could see the diabolical expression on Hitler's face. He was now more convinced than ever that Hitler's face and the face of the man on the incomprehensible machine were the same.

On a rainy Monday, after work, he dropped by the store in Kinsky Palace. Hitler was there, trailing Ottla around like a puppy. While his mother observed them crossly but silently, Hermann Kafka puttered along at work, happy for the presence of an audience who seemed genuinely interested in his tales of poverty and adventure.

When Franz asked to see the sketches he had made on his first outing in the city, Hitler said that he had slept late and then the rain had held him up.

"I decided to come see the palace architecture," he said, "and while I was here I felt obliged to stop in and thank your father for a hearty dinner and a pleasant evenin'."

"This young man knows his architecture," his father said. "You should hear him on the subject. Why, I even learned a few things myself about this very building I rent in."

Franz knew a few things about the palace, too. The upper stories were used as the German Grammar School. He had attended it and, as a result, all that the Kinsky Palace meant to him was the nauseous recollection of Emil Geschwind, God on earth when it came to students and their education. And a vindictive God at that. Now that his father inhabited it, too, Franz had dubbed it "the Nausea Palace" and tried to stay away from it as much as possible. That was one of the reasons his father could never get him near the store—a reason he could never explain because his father wouldn't be interested in hearing it.

But Hitler interested his father. Hermann Kafka leaned over the counter and addressed the young artist with respect:

"So your father was the Imperial Government's Customs Official?"

"Yes sir," Hitler said. "And master of all he surveyed on the Inn River. A very respected man and loved by all. And we had the nicest house in town, too."

"How come you didn't go into the civil service?"

"He wanted me to, but I had a mind of my own."

"They have nice uniforms," Hermann Kafka said. "I've seen them. Wonderfully colorful!"

"My father loved to dress up on the Emperor's birthday."

"I can understand that. Reminds me of my military career. I was in the army, you know. Three years of service when I was nineteen. Came out a *Zugführer*. Loved every minute of it, and learned a lot. I still remember the marching songs."

And then, to the amazement of all, especially his son, Hermann Kafka boomed out in a heavy baritone:

> *"Wann die Soldaten durch die Stadt marchieren*
> *Offnen die Machden die Fenster und die Turen.*
> *Ei warum, ei darum,*
> *Ei warum, ei darum,*
> *Eh, Bloss weg'!*
> *Dem shingdarasse! boomdarasse! shingdara! sa! sa!"*

"Poppa!" Ottla cried. "I didn't know you could sing!"

"You didn't, huh? Well, there's more where that came from!"

Franz didn't want to hear it. He backed out of the store in disbelief and he wasn't missed. His father hadn't mentioned the factory either.

He stood in the rain-soaked square in front of the palace, feeling like an awkward schoolboy who'd had a miserable day at school and now had nothing to look forward to but further unhappiness.

He had a great deal to brood about. If he didn't act wisely and quickly, this intruder was going to be harder and harder to get rid of.

Franz could see him sweet-talking his way into a job at the store, then getting himself a roof over his head, and a chance at Ottla. Since he could not talk to his father, Franz would have to tell Ottla what he suspected. But he knew she would laugh at him if he explained that his warning came from a dream. Ottla did not know or care about dreams as a means of penetrating the secrets of human beings. She was too alive, too spontaneous, too eager to experience each day to try to guess that behind them lay awkward and twisted truths.

Her loving brother was her opposite. Many of his writing ideas came from dreams. He kept notebooks in which he labored to recall detail for detail each chaotic event that ravaged his brain at night. Max was the only one he'd ever shown his notebooks to.

If he told Ottla what he feared, she would say he was acting like a typical big brother. He had done it every other time (Ernst was one of them), so what would be different about the latest attempt to discourage her?

Maybe he should talk to Elli and get her opinion. She had been almost as much a victim of their father's bullying as he was. She married early just to get out of the house away from her tormentor. She was also trying to escape her mother's silent suffering and learned helplessness. She would be able to advise him on how to approach Ottla. There was no need to convince Elli that life was dangerous and that the greatest danger was often from those closest to you. As for his dreams, she would nod her head understandingly.

There was no hope for his father, so Franz was not going to worry about him. He knew his ploys: Hermann Kafka would do anything to ensure that people— customers—knew he was German and not a *pinkeljuden* who had clawed his way out of the ghetto up to middle class respectability. If Hitler had been a Jew, he would have thrown him out of his house and store. But as the son of an important German civil servant—Imperial Customs Official Alois Hitler—this young man was useful. He was a business-minded artist who had bright German dreams dancing in his head. As such, he was welcome at the Kafka home and dry goods store. His spirit was positive. Could his complaining son learn a thing or two from him! And if Franz told his father what he knew about Hitler, Hermann Kafka would scoff and call his son demented.

So it was possible, if Franz weren't careful, for an alliance between his father and sister to form against him. The thought of losing Ottla's loyalty and affection frightened him almost as much as his dreams.

As for his mother, poor woman, the less said to her the better. All she would do is continue to suffer in silence and be obedient to Hermann's wishes. She might withdraw even further behind the wall her husband had erected for her. Valli, having her mother's temperament, would not respond well to her brother's consultation.

He went to see Max at work and told him everything.

Max was skeptical.

"You're not making all of this come true, are you?" Max asked. "Forcing a nightmare to become a reality?"

"You met him, Max. What did you see?"

"An idiot, not worth your thought or mine. A total non-entity. I'm shocked you even brought him around."

"I told you why!" Franz said.

"Yes, my deep dark friend, and if you keep this up you'll go nuts. You ought to reserve your imagination for your writing."

"Maybe he's fooling you because he's fooling himself. Maybe he's unaware. He's the non-entity he seems to be because he's not conscious of the other."

"And only you know the truth?" Max asked. His eyes arched behind his glasses.

"They're my sisters!" Franz cried. "Why shouldn't I be on the look-out for their welfare?"

"But you're endangering them by bringing him around," Max said. "Don't you see? If you had passed him by on the street, he would never have met Ottla! What would the odds be in a city as big as Prague?"

"So what are you saying?" Franz asked. "That I'm causing the danger? That I'm bringing about the very horror I don't want to happen?"

Max grasped his friend's arm.

"Franz! One nightmare! What can it possibly mean? Work on your stories. Work on your God-given gift."

Franz looked at his friend with a sour expression.

"What makes you think it's from God? How do you know it's not from the Devil? Why would God make me suffer the way I do having to pull words out of my brain?"

"It isn't God who makes you suffer, Franz. It's your perfectionism."

Franz stared at his tiny hump-backed friend. He looked even smaller behind his imposing desk. It was even a little comical, but the biggest joke was on him because the tiny man did more writing, got more things published, had more friends, more women, had more life in his twisted body than he would ever have! He didn't know why Max put up with his moods. That trip to Paris would have ended any other friendship. After weeks of cajoling, Max and his brother Otto had finally convinced him to go, and then two days later he broke out in painful boils. He was ruining their vacation until he decided to come back to Prague by himself.

"Maybe I'm Job," Franz said.

Sighing, Max shook his head.

"Don't be Job. Be my brilliant friend. Listen to me and throw that Viennese fake out of your house!"

"He's got my father's ear, now," Franz said. "You should hear the *dreck* that passes between them! He's like a spittoon, you know—a perfectly amiable receptacle for my father's well-aimed squirts of neurosis."

"Why don't you go get him laid and send him home?"

"Do you think that's what he needs?"

"Doesn't everybody? Although I don't know any woman who'd want him in her bed." Then he added: "I can't believe you picked him up like that."

"I told you why."

"Yes, yes."

"You've always encouraged my dreams."

"To write about them, not to live them!"

That reminded him. He had other advice he needed from Max.

"Speaking of writing, you've got to help me with this letter to Dr. Pribram. What kind of tone should I take in it?"

Max threw his arms in the air.

"Franz, are you finished work for the day? I'm not. This may only be the post office, but..."

Franz backed away from the desk.

"Meet me after work," Max said.

"Not at the Arco. I can't stand that place."

"That's where I'm having dinner."

"I don't care," Franz said. "I don't want to go. I can't talk in a crowd. I can't be myself."

"Well, what do you want from me, then? Get rid of Hitler, and just sit down and tell Pribram that you weren't feeling well. He knows you."

"You think so?" Franz put his hand to his brow. "I can't believe what I did."

"So you *did* it!" Max said impatiently. "Now write the letter and forget about it. Speak to his son. Tell him to put a good word in for you. Believe me, it's nothing. Enjoy your promotion instead of agonizing over it."

"I can't."

Max pointed a finger at him.

"So I'm right again. It's your perfectionism. You can't deal with a situation unless conditions are perfect. That's why you're alone all the time—because people aren't perfect."

Franz bowed humbly.

"Thank you, Dr. Freud."

"Well, for God's sake, Franz…"

Chapter Eight

In a disconsolate mood, he walked along the river. There was nowhere to go. He wasn't hungry, he wasn't sleepy, there was no one to talk to. So he walked. An afternoon fog was beginning to give Prague its usual ghostly cast. The sun was simply a round dot in the sky.

Franz crossed the Charles Bridge, walked along the riverbank until he reached the spot where he always moored his dinghy. If he couldn't go for a swim, at least he'd row on the river a bit and think things over.

He took off his hat and jacket, undid his tie and rolled up his sleeves in preparation for his exertion.

Prague, although a large city, became a suburb quickly. Shortly thereafter, the scene was rural.

The foggy city was soon behind him as he rowed along green, misty, and lacey banks. Franz felt better to be away from people, but he did not feel free. What would free him? Impossible question. He hadn't the slightest notion of an answer. Each problem was a door that opened on a second door, then a third, then a fourth, and so on endlessly until you reached the Last Door. No, he did not feel free because he was unloved, and incapable of love himself. That's what was at the bottom of it all.

Max was right about his perfectionism, but he didn't know why he was so obsessed. Nor did Max, who liked to steer clear of blind alleys. Maybe that's why they were inseparable friends. Yin and Yang. They complemented each other. Max was ineffably positive; he was endlessly morbid. Without Max to coax him, encourage him, drive him hopefully forward, he would have plunged out any number of windows or slipped into the Moldau with some heavy rocks in his pockets. How many times had Max intervened, told his parents to stop crowding him and pushing him toward a final plunge. Once he had written Franz's mother a letter, and soon after that his father took some of the pressure off, at least for a while.

Franz was so engrossed in his thoughts that he did not, for a few minutes, notice the banks of the river disappearing from his view. The fog was thickening and he thought it best to tie up by the bank rather than attempt to make it back blindly.

He rowed to a tree limb that jutted out into the river and secured the dinghy to it. Then, lying back in the little boat, he rested, staring dreamily at the fog-enshrouded trees and brush.

Oh, impossible questions, he thought. What would free him? What would abolish his frightening dreams that demanded so much of him during his waking hours? And what must he write to Dr. Pribram to diminish his feeling of humiliation? No matter how many things he did well at the Institute, one slip and he felt he had lost his security. Why couldn't he move away, find a new job, leave Prague altogether for Munich or Berlin or Cologne—real German cities? Why couldn't he move just two miles away, across the river?

Putting his hands over his face, Franz sighed. He shut his eyes, squeezing them tight. As he did so, flashes of light appeared. Then he relaxed his grip on himself, removing his hands from his face and letting his right hand drop into the cool waters of the Moldau. He placed his other hand behind his neck so as to pillow himself on the sharp stern of the dinghy.

A time passed during which he seemed to be dozing when a great sudden shaking of the craft alarmed him. He felt he was going to be pitched into the river. Grasping the sides, he tried to keep the dinghy from overturning, but the shaking got worse and the line snapped off the tree. Before he could do anything about it, he was floating in the fog with a giant of a man sitting in the bow, facing him. His horrible face was livid with anger; his teeth were bared; his eyes cold. He was wearing the rough clothing of a prison inmate, striped in gray and white. On his feet were hobnailed boots. When the ugly thing turned around, Franz observed a six-pointed yellow star on its back. Was he human? Franz thought so at first; yet, no. There was something too horrifying about him to be human.

He looked around for a weapon. Picking up an oar, he raised it threateningly.

"Drop it!" the thing said matter-of-factly. "It won't do you any good. Anyway, I'm here to talk to you; nothing more. We're both Prager citizens."

"You're from Prague?" Franz asked, slowly replacing the oar.

"Deep in the heart of it. I'm the Golem."

Franz' heart froze.

"The Golem!"

"Yes," the thing said.

"Who's been dead for centuries?"

"Resting, not dead. Lying in wait. Anticipating. Waiting for a man…"

"Who? What man?" Franz said.

"I'll get to that."

Franz shrank his body as far into the corner of the dinghy as he could.

"Where did you come from?"

"Where I live. In the attic of the Old Synagogue."

Franz's eyes bulged gray and watery.

"But..."

"Don't be afraid. Fear is not what I want from you. Let's talk," the Golem said. "You mustn't fear *me*."

The tone of his voice turned sad, but the expression on his face remained the same, and it remained the same regardless of the sound of his voice. It was as if he had a mask on, but there seemed to be no evidence of a mask. It was an ugly human face fixed permanently into an expression of blazing anger. It was impossible for Franz to look at the Golem for more than a few seconds at a time.

"That's all right," the Golem said. "Look away. You can't hurt my feelings. I've been alone in that attic for hundreds of years. Look at the river and the trees. Keep your eye on something pleasant."

The Golem put a wretched hand in the water and swirled it.

"Nice," he said. He took his hand out and let water dribble on his brow. "Four hundred years in the dust. But I kept in touch; I've seen what's been going on, and yet no one's seen fit to put the *shem* back in my mouth. Only Rabbi Loew was courageous enough. But he had his limits, the old rabbi."

"What brought you out?" Franz asked.

The Golem put his hand back in the water.

"Let's say circumstances did. A terrible crisis. I can't find words strong enough to express what I know and feel."

He took his hand out of the water again and touched his neck.

"I haven't got all day, Dr. Kafka. The fog will be lifting soon and you don't want people to see me rowing along with you, do you? We might attract some attention."

"Is this a dream?" Franz asked. "Am I dreaming?"

"No."

The Golem cupped his hand and brought water out of the river.

"Is it still drinkable? It *was*, four hundred years ago. You could see clear to the bottom. I can't see the bottom now."

He drank.

"An improvement over dust," he said.

He wiped his stiff unyielding mouth.

"You are in crisis," Dr. Kafka. You put the *shem* back in my mouth. You made me stir to life the other day in your thoughts. You uttered a simple sentence and I awoke after four hundred years."

"What did I say?" Franz asked.

"You said you had nothing in common with Jews, and you denied your identity with the man in the street. The expression on my face is the response of your ancestors. You have deadened your own heart."

"Pardon me, sir," Franz said, offended.

The Golem put his hand forward and suddenly Franz was in darkness.

"You had a dream the other night that your sisters faced extinction. I have awakened to tell you that you are a man of destiny."

"Me?"

Through all of his terror, Franz couldn't help laughing.

"A man of destiny? Mr. Golem, undoubtedly, you've come to the wrong man."

"The wrong man is always the right man," the Golem said softly, having put his hand back in the water.

"I can't look at your face," Franz said.

"My face is your lost self, that's why you can't bear to look at me. My face is your anger, your abandoned power. I've come to make you act."

"You've made a mistake," Franz said. "You've made a big mistake." And then the sentence was out of his mouth and coming from another source.

"YOU'VE MADE A MISTAKE TO TIE YOUR BOAT TO MY FAVORITE TREE!" a vagabond was shouting from the river bank. Franz awoke and saw a demented hobo waving him away from the bank of the river, apparently his personal property.

Franz found his oars and began rowing back to the city.

"DON'T MAKE THAT MISTAKE AGAIN, IF YOU KNOW WHAT'S GOOD FOR YOU!" he was warned as the figure and the riverbank disappeared in the fog.

Chapter Nine

Walking back across the river, Franz saw that the fog had rolled on and the sun was beginning to drench the bridge in light. He was happy to be among people again, feeling that his encounter-dream had gone on for hours instead of minutes.

He stopped in the middle of the bridge and looked at the Moldau. Was the Golem nearby? Had anybody seen him? Had the statues on the bridge, which saw everything that happened in Prague, had they observed this massive, ugly figure cross over from the Old Town? Maybe he flew. Maybe he materialized and de-materialized at will. Had no one in the Synagogue heard the commotion made by the rising of a four-hundred-year-old corpse?

Another dream. Another part of the pattern. Another warning. What was he going to do about it?

Rather than going home, he decided to go back to the office and write that miserable letter of apology to Dr. Pribram and get the whole thing off his mind.

As he climbed to his office on the fifth floor of the Institute, he found himself explaining to colleagues who knew he got off at two P.M. that he had forgotten some papers and had come to collect them. He looked at his co-workers sheepishly, like a little boy who'd forgotten his homework. They said, "Ah, Franz," and "Oh, Dr. Kafka," to the kindly and friendly legal counselor in the accident section.

He sat at his desk, took paper from a drawer and a pen from the desktop. He wrote: "Dear Dr. Pribram," and, then for a few minutes, nothing else. His hand was rigid above the paper as he tried to force an apology, but instead of writing he started doodling, then sketching. He drew the Golem's ghastly face and attached to it a stiff massive body. Next to the Golem's he drew Hitler's face. The more he worked on the thin papery look, the less wan it appeared. Franz's stroke became heavier and heavier until the second sketch was not much different from the first. What had the Golem said? Something about, "My face is your lost anger, your abandoned power. I've come to make you act." Well, if that were the case, why couldn't he write a simple letter of apology to Pribram? It was a simple act. But Franz knew why he was paralyzed. He had no desire to apologize. That's what his father has been expecting all these years, what all fathers expect because of their so-called exalted position.

"Dear Dr. Pribram" was already too much. He was a pompous man, filled with self-importance, eminence, and dignity, certain of who he was, certain of his role, a man who thought his life contained no risks and was accident-free. It was the falsity of it all that made Franz resist. Dr. Pribram had create a wall around himself, he had wrapped himself in a vision of stability and permanence at the Accident Institute that could be damaged, invaded, exploded in any second by any number of blows, but he never seemed aware of the possibilities. There was never an appearance of vulnerability in him or Hermann Kafka. Why was he—Franz—the vulnerable one?

The Golem was another problem: the fixity of expression, the rage, the never-ceasing anger, the one, sole expression. And Franz's dream only wanted one thing from him—to get rid of this thing from Vienna, this pathetic, uneducated hick from the backwoods. All he had to do to save his sisters was obey.

Frustrated, he ripped up the pages he had sketched, threw them away, and sank back in his chair. He thought of the shop girl he used for his pleasure. He needed her. He needed her very badly.

It was dark when he got to Zeltnergasse. As he climbed the stairs, he heard his father singing again. Another army song!

> *Morgen marchieren Wir*
> *Durch dem Feld zum haupt Quartier,*
> *Eine Tasse Tee*
> *Zucker und Café*
> *Und ein Glaschen Wein.*

He heard stomping and imagined his father marching around the house. It could only mean one thing: he was showing off to Hitler, telling his military stories again. Was Ottla there, too, entranced by the watery blue eyes of the postcard painter?

"It's a mighty army we have," Hermann Kafka expounded after observing his son's quiet entrance. "Discipline, order, efficiency. If we ever get into a war, we'll surprise everybody because we are ready! More than ready! Listen, I've still got the *esprit de corps* from twenty years ago!"

He sang the song again, pounding his fists on the table as Franz went by. Ottla was laughing, but it wasn't her usual laughter of ridicule.

Franz was impressed by something. She liked seeing this side of her father. It made Franz sick, and he was ready to go out again, at any minute, as soon as he could think of an excuse.

"Dr. Kafka," Hitler said, "your father has wonderful stories about his Army exploits."

"Yes, I know," Franz said gloomily. "How is your sketching coming, by the way?"

"Not too well," Hitler said. "Did you see that fog today? I was trying to sketch the Kinsky Palace and I was suddenly lost in it."

"Did you go anywhere else?"

"No. I didn't have the chance."

"This man is good," Hermann Kafka said, "very good. When he sketches a building, he puts in every detail, so you know exactly what building it is. It's better than sketching."

"He's very good," Ottla said.

"Thank you," Hitler said. "Now if I can convince my buyers in Vienna, I'll be doin' all right."

"It's good to meet an ambitious man," Hermann Kafka said. "I understand ambition. The young people today are all talk and no action. I believe in action."

Franz knew these opinions were meant for him. He turned away.

"The young people today don't have the energy we did. Do you agree, Herr Hitler? More schnapps, Herr Hitler? I started with nothing and now I've the best dry good store in Prague. And an asbestos factory!"

He threw a hard look at his son.

"As long as people keep their promises and fulfill their responsibilities, things will go well. Did you hear your father talk this way, Herr Hitler?"

"Occasionally," Hitler said, "but most of the time he was out on business."

"Yes, yes," Herman Kafka agreed. "My generation was an active one."

"I'm going over to Max's," Franz said. Then turning to Hitler, "Do you think you can get back to your hostel by yourself?"

Hitler organized himself.

"Are you leaving? I'd better go back with you, Dr. Kafka. These alleys at night make me uneasy. You don't know how many times I've been threatened in Vienna."

"Can I come?" Ottla said.

"No," Franz said fiercely. "I told you I'm going to Max's."

There it was again. Ottla was more than curious about this anemic specimen.

Hermann Kafka put up his meaty hand.

"You're not going anywhere, young lady. I want that store opened on time tomorrow morning."

Franz could see his sister suppressing her anger; he could feel her embarrassment. Without a stranger present, Ottla would have lashed out at his father and there would have been a few minutes of verbal war before her mother's teary appeals and his father's determination got the best of her.

"I just want to see Max, too," she said.

Franz was amused. Ottla had about as much interest in seeing Max right now as Franz did. All he wanted to do is get out of the house and away from his father. All Ottla wanted to do is spend a little more time with this Viennese *schnorrer*. Why? What was his appeal?

Chapter Ten

"You have a wonderful family," Hitler said as they walked through the night towards the Old Town Square. "It makes me remember what it was to have a family. A German without his family is a man without limbs."

Franz wondered if Hitler was being serious or if he was subtly mocking him. Could he have missed the constant hostility that caused so much gloom in the Kafka household?

"I had a saint for a mother," Hitler said. "That's the only way to describe her. Always loving, always concerned, always there. Your mother reminds me of her."

"I see," Franz said cautiously, convinced that he must not expose his true feelings to a man who blubbered like this.

"She didn't have much luck, but she was a brave woman right to the end."

"You have no other family now?"

"No, I was the only one, my mother's darling. I drew a picture of her when she died. Her body was emaciated, but she was still beautiful."

A sob caught in Hitler's throat. Franz heard grief in this sound.

"Her eyes expressed her soul. They were blue and they glowed with a mother's love."

Franz was almost touched by this man's sentimentality. Germans were like that.

"I've got my mother's eyes, but my father's temper," Hitler said. "She used to call me her little Indian because I was such a rowdy boy. If I wasn't out in the woods leadin'

74

a hunting party, I was hidin' from my old... the old gentleman. She was a dear, wonderful woman."

Franz thought of his own weak little mother. Would he ever be able to generate that kind of love for her? He felt uncomfortable being touched by Hitler's emotions.

"When I buried her, I buried a great part of myself."

With a shiver, Hitler came out of a momentary trance and looked around at the dark streets.

"I'd never have found my way by myself," he said. "Why is it so dark? You'd think there'd be some lights. Is this a Jew neighborhood?"

"Yes."

"I'm surprised your father would put up with them."

"He wants to be near his business."

"True," Hitler said, "so they don't steal from him."

"Does my father remind you of yours?" Franz asked.

"Yes and no," Hitler said. "Your father seems to be a gentler man."

"Gentler?"

"I mean, behind his gruffness, there's a certain..."

"What?"

"...warmth, I would call it. He's good company."

"How was your father different?"

"There was no warmth," Hitler said. "He was the Customs Inspector all the time. He was never out of uniform. That's why I'll never become a bureaucrat."

"If he were alive now, what would he say to your choice of career?"

"He'd run me out of the house. I'd have to be farther away from him than Vienna. You couldn't argue with my father; you just listened."

"So you're all alone in Vienna," Franz pursued.

"Yes."

"Do you have any girlfriends?"

"Well, I have… some… acquaintances," Hitler explained. "I have a partner."

"Do you see women?"

"See?"

"Consort with them."

"Consort?"

Hitler was getting confused, tongue-tied.

"Go with them?" Franz said.

"Go with?"

"Fuck them!"

"Oh, my God," Hitler shut his eyes and put his hands to his lips.

"I'm sorry," Franz said.

"No… no…"

"I'm only trying to…"

"That's all right. I'm not used…"

"Do you go to brothels?"

"Well, ah…"

"I'm not trying to embarrass you," Franz said.

"Oh… I know…"

"Do you need a woman? That's all I meant. I can help you. We use brothels here. Didn't your father…"

"My father?"

''Am I offending you?"

"No, but…"

"You spoke of so much loneliness," Franz said, "I simply thought I could help. I know some girls—shop girls, maids, very nice…"

Hitler's face roved the dark street looking for escape, some new point of attention. Franz was convinced that he had a real rube on his hands who hardly knew which end was up. Just what were his dreams trying to tell him?

"In Linz, we…we moved to Linz…there were no… brothels."

"But Vienna has much to offer," Franz said.

"Opera," Hitler said.

"I wasn't thinking of opera."

"I go to the opera all the time."

"I don't know much about that subject," Franz said.

"It's my home."

"The Vienna Opera?"

"Yes. My spiritual home."

"Wagner?"

"Yes," Hitler said, breathing more easily. "A true genius."

"I've never seen a Wagner opera."

"But you've heard…"

"Only a little."

"To see and hear Wagner in the Vienna Opera amid the glory of the Ringstrasse!"

Hitler had found his voice again. He drew himself erect, casting off the dark cloak that Franz was trying to rope him in.

"I spend everything I have to go. Sometimes I go without food. I've seen *Tristan Und Isolde* thirty times."

"Thirty times! That must be a record. I'll bet Wagner didn't see it that often."

"Well, I have," Hitler said, "and I'll see it thirty more."

They were alone in the narrowing streets of the Old Town.

"We're coming to the synagogue where the Golem I told you about is sleeping," Franz said.

They had reached the edge of the Old Town Square. Franz pointed across it to the old synagogue.

"I haven't forgotten the story you told me about," Hitler said. "Could his bones still be there?"

"Still there," Franz said, "awaiting resurrection to save the Jews from persecution."

A look of disgust crossed Hitler's face.

"Does anyone ever go up there to…"

"Only those with knowledge of the *Cabbala*," Franz said, amusing himself with his invention.

"The what?"

"You've never heard of the *Cabbala*?"

"No" Hitler said. "Never."

"It's Jewish mysticism," Franz said suppressing a grin. "In order to be redeemed and find unity with God, the Cabbalists study the unknown, they talk to the dead, they search for the means to change metals into gold."

"My God!"

"They say that the Book of the *Cabbala* is the secret wisdom stretching all the way back to Adam."

"How different Jews are," Hitler said. "How primitive."

"That's why they're kept in ghettos," Franz said.

"Surely."

"They're not like us Germans; they lack clear-sightedness."

"They frighten me in Vienna," Hitler said.

"Vienna has no Golem."

"Was he actually made from clay by the rabbi?"

"Absolutely! For revenge!"

"Will he appear again?"

"When the Jews are ready for revenge," Franz said, finding it hard to restrain his laughter.

Hitler turned his synagogue-fixed gaze to Franz.

"I've never heard of any of this, but I've felt it a hundred times walking among them—their clothes, their hair, their smells, their…"

"…unworldliness?" Franz added gleefully.

"Yes, that's it."

"They speculate endlessly while living in shame. The Cabbalists even disobey the Talmud."

"They look like savages."

"They're so engaged in thought, even their underwear shows. They go against the Talmudic law by asking what is above, what is beneath, what was before, and what will be hereafter."

"It's outrageous," Hitler said. "In Linz there were a few of them, but Vienna…!"

"They knew their place in Linz, I'll bet," Franz said.

"Certainly. Except for their noses, you might even say they were like us. Nothing like Vienna. Nothing!"

Franz wished he had a key to the synagogue so that he could take him up to see the bones of the Golem. He would want Max to be there as a witness.

And also Yitzak Levi. He, most of all. Why, he'd make an outrageous skit of it, and put it into one of his plays at the Yiddish theater. Oh, to have Yitzak here! Bumbling Jew meets Stumbling German! Golem meets Austrian hick and doesn't know what to make of him. Golem meets Wagner and they sing a duet. Golem meets the Forest Dweller and they have Sex in a Tree. Wagner plays the Cabbala—Audience walks out!

Yitzak Levi, nemesis of Hermann Kafka, would have them all rolling in the aisles. He might even make Hitler laugh. Yes, he could cool hot German blood with jokes, songs, and his irrepressible joyous *yiddishkeit*:

I'm Yitzak Levi, I ain't no heavy,
I like to dance and joke and prance around and sing.
I'm Yitzak Levi, a schlep from Schvevy,
A crazy ghetto nut who wouldn't be a king!

I know the Golem; his name is Yohlem,
He's such a dear he wouldn't even hurt a flea,
He loves the Germans, he loves the Poles,
And I even speculate that he loves me!

He eats Cabbala; he thinks it's salad!
He even masticates a frau or two!
Don't get him angry! Don't get him mad!
Because he even might consider eating you!

That Hermann Kafka, he doesn't like me,
That's why his son invites me all the time.
Makes Hermann jumpy and very grumpy,
He says, "This Yid is sure no friend of mine!"

As they crossed the Square in silence, each deep in his own thoughts, Franz was again pricked by the recollection of his dreams. Yet he couldn't understand just what danger this helpless man could possibly be. There was a mistake somewhere, some error in communication or transmission, from above or below that he did not understand, some evasiveness impossible to trap. Still, for his sisters' sake, he had to keep up the pursuit.

"I guess you'll be happy to get back to Vienna," Franz said, resuming the conversation.

"The only reason I have to go back is my business and the opera," Hitler said.

"You make me feel that I've really missed something in my life," Franz said. "The only music I know is what they play at the Yiddish theater."

"If it weren't for the opera, I couldn't have survived Vienna," Hitler said. "Do you feel that way about anythin'? I don't get the feelin' you would."

"I do, though," Franz said.

"What about?"

"Writing."

"Yes, you said so. You understand how I feel, then. When I… Can I speak frankly?"

"Of course."

"When I'm sittin' there amid that architectural glory, I begin to quiver inside. When Isolde is waitin' for her lover and the music pulses, I'm not the same man who walked into that theater. I'm a Wagnerian. I'm transformed. It's hard to put that into words."

Hitler's hands went up toward the black sky. They waved like a conductor's. He emitted something like musical sounds.

"The prelude to the third act is the loneliest music ever created. It's a nightmare of loneliness. It is a nightmare. Tristan is dyin' of his wounds at his deserted castle in Brittany. He is guarded by Kurvenal who has sent for Isolde so that they might have a last reunion. But it's too late. Tristan dies just as Isolde reaches him. And for Isolde, the last hour has come, too. This is the Love-Death."

"The Love-Death?" Franz said skeptically.

"If you've never heard it, Dr. Kafka, prepare yourself for a glimpse of eternity. To Tristan and Isolde, day is evil, it is the time of men, it is action and responsibility, it draws them apart. But night… It's the night they long for, the blissful realm of night:

81

O now we are to night devoted,
The dishonest day, with envy bloated,
Lying, could not mislead,
Though it might part us, indeed!

I wish I had the voice to sing it for you.

All the day's gleams in flashes outblazing
Blind our eyes no more.
Those who death's dark night boldly survey,
Those who have studied her secret way,
The daylight's falsehood..."

"The mysteries of the *Cabbala*," Franz taunted.

"The what, sir?" Hitler exploded, cutting his hands out of mid-air.

"It sounds a little like the *Cabbala* I was telling you about."

Hitler's body, which talk of Wagner had made rigid and reaching, now seemed to collapse from this odious, disturbing reference.

"I know there is no way without seeing an actual performance to understand the genius of the man. Wagner gives us eternity. He lets us know it's there, and I have never felt it more than in his works."

Jews and women, Franz was thinking. This fellow has plenty of trouble with Jews and women. As long as he can fantasize, he's all right. Let's get him off his Wagnerian pedestal.

"Wouldn't you like a real woman, tonight?" Franz asked.

"Sir?"

Crash went the pedestal.

"You talk a lot about abstractions. What about real people? Real women?"

"I'll marry when my artistic talent has been recognized."

"That could be a long time," Franz said. "I'm talking about a real woman—tonight!"

"I couldn't possibly," Hitler said, making reference to something about himself by touching his hand to his chest in an unconscious way.

"These girls are good," Franz said. "They're professionals."

"I must..." Hitler turned away. "I've got to get my work done."

"You don't want to let Wagner ruin your sex life," Franz said.

"How could he?" Hitler asked like a boy.

"There's so much time you can spend in an opera house."

"Nothing can equal that experience."

"Want to try?"

"Please," Hitler said courteously, "I can get to the hostel from here. I've taken up too much of your time already."

Franz watched him walk off unsteadily in the dark. He made a wrong turn and Franz had to call out and tell him how to proceed.

He was pleased that he had intimidated him with the offer of sex. And yet Hitler had looked at Ottla with great interest. Franz had felt a rapacity in his stare. Was he willing to use his own sister as bait to trap the scourge of his dreams? Some scourge. All he could do so far was turn up an effete, helpless, south German artist, a man lost in the big city, a man unfit for the struggle of life, bawling over his past, mooning over Tristan and Isolde.

That night at the hostel, Hitler had a dream. He was with a girl and he was enjoying her company very much. They walked along on a summer's evening and visited an amusement park. They were enjoying themselves when a group of men singled him out and separated him from the girl, who looked like Ottla. He ran after her but he lost her as she disappeared among some loathsome, dirty people. He didn't want to pursue her for fear of getting himself covered with filth. He boarded a special train and rode through town making all the people board his train in the hope that one of them would be the girl. But all he collected were ugly people.

When he returned home from his visit to the shop-girl, Franz wrote the following in his diary:

"From the viewpoint of literature, my fate is simple. The urge to depict my dreamlike inner life has thrust everything into the background; and now someone steps out of my dreams and into my life and what must I do? While my life seems to shrink, something else—a warning—thrusts me forward into action, and I am helpless. This man. What am I to do about him? With each passing day, he intrudes into our lives, but I gave him permission to intrude. I must have more evidence. Dreams are not enough, even the dream of The Thing that assaulted me on the Moldau."

Chapter Eleven

With a plan in mind, Franz and Max went to see Yitzak Levi. Franz had thought of it while exercising at his window.

He had met Zak by accident about two years before when Max had all but forced him to go to the dumpy Café Savoy to see a Yiddish theater group perform. It was called The Polish Yiddish Travelling Theater Company. Its stage was nothing more than a corner of the greasy restaurant.

Zak was the lively leader of the troupe of eight which had gotten stuck in Prague when its funds ran low. Franz didn't know why he consented to see these players. It certainly wasn't because he was attracted to Yiddish art. Thanks to his father, there wasn't anything Jewish that caught his fancy or aroused his interest. Sometimes, to pacify his mother, he went to the Altneu synagogue on the Day of Atonement. He always went away irritated with Jewish behavior. In his diary, he had written:

"Churchlike interior. Muted stock exchange mutterings. Three orthodox, presumably eastern Jews in socks, bent over their prayer books, prayer shawls pulled up over their heads, becoming as small as possible. Two of them weeping. A lot of noise. The family of a brothel-owner came in. A small boy is pushing his way through the congregation. A man who looks like a clerk is shaking himself briskly while he prays, trying to put the strongest possible emphasis on each word, creating even more noise."

Still, he found Zak attractive even though he was talking and singing that fascinating Yiddish, while acting in a lowbrow tearjerker.

Franz and Max stayed after the performance and met Zak and the troupe. Franz found him to be an intelligent actor with a delightfully outgoing personality. He was friendly and colorful. He seemed to be free of self-absorption and brooding inwardness. These characteristics disarmed Franz and so what appeared to be a burden became an enjoyable evening. Max had been right again.

Zak's frank accounts of his life and travels also captivated Franz. He had rebelled against his orthodox family when he was seventeen, fled Warsaw and ended up in Paris as a fledging actor in amateur Yiddish production companies. Soon he joined a professional theater group and began acting and singing in all the major Jewish population centers in Europe.

This was the kind of life that Franz would only fantasize about. Rebel. Flee. Run like hell from family clutches. See the world. But not the Jewish world. Not for him.

Brave fellow, Yitzak Levi.

Stuck in Prague, Yitzak fastened himself onto these curious intellectuals. So what if they were slumming. They came to his theater. The more people he met, the more help might come his way, the quicker he'd be able to get his troupe on the road again. Anyway, he wasn't overwhelmed by these bright boys. He'd been around and seen plenty, whereas they got what they knew out of books.

Soon he was fast friends with Max and Franz. He spent afternoons at the Kafka house, but not evenings because he knew that Hermann Kafka was an anti-Semite who thought Levi was a *meshuggene ritoch* and a totally useless person. Hermann warned his son that if he lay down with dogs, he was going to get fleas.

Zak also went on long walks with Franz and Ottla.

86

"Franz," he chirped, "you got a problem with the old man? Let ole Zakkie help you with it. There's nothing I wouldn't do for you because I know what you're going through. Ain't parents a bitch? Why do you think I ran away from them? All that suffocating so-called love." Zak contorted his handsome face. "Nyyyaaaaggghhh."

Franz revealed his plan.

"Zak, can you do me a favor? Do you have a play...?"

"Do I have a play? Does a cow have milk? Does a kitchen have a sink?"

"I'm serious," Franz said. "Do you have a play about assimilation problems?"

"Does a bear shit in the woods? Sure. Hundreds... and one in particular I can think of."

"What's it about? Can you put it on?"

"Sure," Zak said, "but what's the angle?"

"I've got a friend, a German friend, who's kind of naïve. He's never met any Jews and we got to talking about the question of assimilation, and I thought if you had a play in your repertoire..."

"I got a play, but what's with your friend, he never met a Jew?"

"Well, he's from the backwoods. He's new in Prague and I thought it would help him if he got a look at Yiddish theater."

"It's all right with me," Zak said, "as long as you promise to bring along that sweet sister of yours."

"I can arrange that," Franz said.

"Good. We've got a play called "Possessed." It's the story of two Jewish families, the Seidmanns and the Edelmanns, both rich guys. Siedmann wants to get assimilated so he gets himself baptized. In order to

87

convince the goys that he's for real, he publicly expresses disgust for everything Jewish."

"Sounds like someone I know," Franz said.

"When his wife refuses to be baptized, he poisons her, and he gets away with it."

"Are you sure the play won't start a riot?"

"Naw, don't worry," Zak said. "It's got a happy ending."

"Hmmmm."

"Well, the poisoned wife happens to be the sister of Edelmann who is a rich moneylender about to emigrate to Palestine. A German officer, who owes Edelmann a lot of money, wants to marry Seidmann's daughter. Seidmann of course approves, but the daughter is in love with Edelmann's son who's faithful to Judaism. This upsets Seidmann, especially when his daughter goes over to Judaism, even though she had been forcibly baptized. The thing is she can't marry young Edelmann because she's officially a Christian.

"Seidmann, being a shrewd duck, gives his blessing to the marriage, lures the elder Edelmann to his house under the pretext of paying off the German officer's debts, and stabs him to death. Seidmann arranges things so that suspicion falls on the young Edelmann. He's arrested.

"The German officer now has a clear shot at Seidmann's daughter and Seidmann is very pleased at the way things have turned out. But one night, the ghost of Edelmann appears in his house and demands justice. His wife appears, too, and Seidmann thinks he's going crazy. He promises, if the ghosts will stop haunting him, to give half his fortune to the Jewish community. Then he demands to see God to justify himself.

"Meanwhile, Seidmann's daughter lures the German officer to her bed and kills him as they make love. God rejects Seidmann's explanations, foretells his doom, and orders him as a last act of courage to return to Judaism and free his daughter to marry young Edelmann. God lets him live just long enough to see his daughter's marriage. The play ends. You'll enjoy it; it's funny."

"Funny?"

"Oh, sure," Zak said. "We throw in some songs and do a couple of cute skits. We can't get too serious, you know. After all, this is Yiddish theater. There's a lot of black humor in it. One funny bit is that the German officer and the young Edelman are played by the same actor."

"What's funny about that?"

"Where's your sense of humor, Franz? The aggressive German and the pious Jew played by the same actor? That's not funny? I bet your German friend'll get it."

"We'll see."

"Anyway, I've got a theory about Jews and Germans; they're like twins that have to struggle with each other for survival. They're opposite sides of the same coin and the question is who's gonna end face up? A director I met in Paris told me to read a story by Edgar Allan Poe called *William Wilson*. D'ja ever read it?"

"No."

"It's about the deadly double; he says it fits Jews and Germans. But why look at things negatively? I believe in happy endings, so I go along with Heine's prediction that Germans and Jews will become reconciled and build a new Jerusalem in Germany."

"What happens to the rivalry?"

"It turns to love and they all intermarry."

"Some Jew you are!" Franz said, amused.

89

"Why not?" Zak said, putting his arm on Franz's shoulder. "Let's all survive together and put on plays and dance and sing and have a good time. We pass through once; we're entitled to a good time."

"Once is too much," Franz said.

"That's no way to look at it," Zak said, patting Franz's back.

"By the way," Franz said, without acknowledging his friend's optimism, "this friend I'm bringing along doesn't know that I'm a Jew, so if you meet him, don't say anything. Okay?"

"Sure. Everybody I know plays that game."

"Now, is the German officer condemned by the Jews in the play? Are Germans denounced?"

"Not particularly."

"Could I add some lines, just for that one performance?"

"No problem," Zak said. "I always change lines around, just to keep from being bored."

"Good. I'll write them out for you."

"As long as you bring Otta along, I'll say them for you. What's this fellow's name, anyway, that you're bringing along?"

"Hitler," Franz said. "Adolf Hitler."

"That's Jewish, that name," Zak said, probing his memory. "I've run across that name in the ghettos—Hitler, Heidler, Huttler, Hitlermann, all kinds of versions."

"This fellow's from Austria, a kind of Bohemian-artist type."

"What's he doing in Prague?"

"Oh, he paints postcards for the tourist trade."

"Maybe he's a Jew and doesn't want *you* to know?"

90

"No. He's no Jew. He never met one till he got to Vienna."

"And now he's hanging around with the Kafkas," Zak laughed. "That's pretty funny."

Chapter Twelve

At the office, Franz still could not write his letter of apology to Dr. Pribram. He tried again and again to excuse his deplorable conduct, but the words would not flow, would not appear. His growing obsession with Hitler was interfering with his concentration.

He asked Karl Blau to draft a letter. Only after pleading with him did Karl agree. He knew Karl did not have his kind of conscience and that meant, of course, that he would never be precise enough to satisfy Franz. But at least it removed one burden for the time being.

With his plan ripening, Franz was hoping he would get a strong signal, an absolute signal that Hitler was the man he must act against to protect his sisters. Stopping by the store on his way home, he was again surprised to see Hitler there, engaged in conversation with Ottla. Franz could see she was enjoying it.

His father was in a good mood, too, but as soon as he saw his son, his expression soured and he started in on Franz's laziness and his failure to supervise at the factory.

Franz tried to ignore his father. He inquired as to how many sketches Hitler had made. He was shocked to hear Hitler answer in an almost cavalier way, as if he were the secure one and Franz the intruder.

"Not many yet. I've decided to spend more time in Prague," Hitler said.

"Good, good," Hermann said. "Prague has much to offer. You really need more time."

Franz had never heard a word of encouragement from his father, but here he was now, inviting a stranger to cuddle up with the Kafkas.

"I've an idea," Franz said. "Why don't we go to the theater tonight?"

"Oh, that's a good idea," Ottla said merrily. "What'll we see?"

"Something that will really bring the flavor of Prague across," Franz said.

"There's an Arthur Schnitzler play on," Ottla said.

"We'll talk about it later over dinner," Franz said. "Let's go out and eat."

"But your mother's making a big spread," Hermann said with disappointment.

"Maybe tomorrow night," Franz said. "That all right with you, Alf?"

"I certainly don't mind, as long as Mr. Kafka..."

"Go ahead, go ahead," the father waved with an angry look at his son. "Enjoy yourselves."

At dinner, they made plans.

"The Yiddish Theater," Franz announced.

"Oh, goodie," Ottla said. "We'll see Zak."

Hitler took notice; his eyes widened.

"Yiddish? I don't... I have no knowledge of..."

"That's no problem," Franz said. "I'll interpret for you."

"My brother's a linguist," Ottla said with perfect timing, as if she knew of the plot.

"In Prague, you have to be," Franz said. "Germans, Czechs, Gypsies, Jews..."

"I think I'd prefer the Schnitzler play," Hitler said.

Franz was prepared for this. He despised Schnitzler's plays, thought they were sickening drivel.

"Oh, I checked," Franz said, "and they're not giving it tonight."

"Don't worry, Alf," Ottla said, "You'll love it. Zak's a terrific actor."

"Zak?" Hitler said, aware of the nickname.

"Yitzak Levi. He's the head of the Polish Yiddish Traveling Company. He's wonderful. You'll like him."

"He calls himself 'the Yid from Warsaw'," Franz said.

"I...I... think I told you," Hitler began. "Do... do... do you remember?"

"Ah, yes, the stink and the dirt, Franz said. "Nothing to worry about. These Jews are clean and funny."

"Trust us," Ottla said, reaching out and touching Hitler's arm.

"It's... just that... Vienna is a part of me. I can't get it out of my head—the drunken wreck at the next table, the crook who sold me a used razor blade for a new one, the child with vermin crawlin' down his neck in broad daylight..."

"Prague's different," Ottla said.

Chapter Thirteen

At the Café Savoy, Hitler sat between Franz and Ottla. Franz pulled his chair forward so that when he translated for Hitler, he would be able to see his full expression.

"Why are they usin' a restaurant?" Hitler asked.

"Well, this isn't your traditional theater," Franz said.

"When I go to the theater in Vienna..." Hitler began.

"This isn't Vienna or Wagner," Franz interrupted. "It's makeshift theater, make-do theater, but the content is good and the language is unique. Yiddish is a language always threatened with destruction, but it keeps on flowering. There's a saying that goes—Yiddish has been in trouble for the last five hundred years, and it will still be in trouble for the next thousand."

Hitler focussed his eyes on the tiny stage. Here, now, as the lights went down, was the test. Hitler's face darkened; Franz glimpsed anxiety. Hitler's fists tightened; Franz glimpsed rage.

He was as close to Hitler's ear as a lover would be. An occasional shaft of warm breath made Hitler's head move backwards. The onions on Franz's breath made the head stagger, the eyes smart, the fists clench. "Possession" had begun and Franz translated, embroidered, digressed, invented. Ottla, surprised at her brother's behavior, looked at him in confusion, but various eye signals from him kept her quiet.

He gave each caricature on stage a diabolical motive. He assured Hitler that Seidmann assimilated into Christianity in order to steal from all Germans, to use Jewish tricks and lack of morality to rob honest German businessmen. He described the elder Edelmann as a Jewish nationalist who, through usury, would cheat Germans out of their money and then use it in Palestine to build a Jewish state.

Franz described the German officer as a pawn, easily manipulated by Seidmann because of the officer's sense of duty and honor.

"He's a farmer's boy," Franz told him, "who through hard work has won his commission. He has no idea of deceit and corruption. He loves Seidmann's daughter with the kind of purity of feeling that only a German can feel for his "Mutter." The Jews have no conception of "Mutter." There is a sense of loving Christian splendor in the sound. A Jew despoils the term when he uses it.

"Now under orders from the evil father, the innocent girl uses her overly-endowed body to seduce the German officer against his training and belief, and, at the moment of his climax, cuts off his genitals."

An inhuman force seemed to yank Hitler out of his seat, tear him from Franz's lips and catapult him out of the Savoy into the street. Franz was right behind him, ordering Ottla to go back and watch the play. Facing more Jews in the street, Hitler found a dark alley where he could hide. His breath was rapid, his face full of sweat, his eyes wide with panic.

Franz touched his arm solicitously.

"What is it, Alf?" he asked. "What happened?"

"I can't... I can't... breathe. My God, that place!"

"What about it?"

"I knew... I knew I shouldn't have come! How could you bring me here? These vermin... these... beasts!"

Franz professed innocence.

"It's just a play. You should..."

"No! No!" Hitler shouted. "I can't stand it! I told you about Vienna. It's just like Vienna. Didn't I tell you? I used to get sick to my stomach from the smell. I told you that. The way they dressed, the way they looked, the way they talked…"

He held his hand to his mouth, turned aside and vomited. Franz did not turn away, but watched with fascination as the plenteous gobbets of food and drink poured from Hitler's Jew-ridden body. He spattered his pants and shoes.

"I'm sorry," Franz said. "Let me help you."

"It's not your fault," Hitler said, heaving and gagging. "I shoulda known this would happen. I shouldn't have come."

"Forgive me," Franz said.

"That talk about a German mother," Hitler panted. "God help me."

He began to sob. He was totally wretched now. Franz gave him his handkerchief with which he covered his eyes.

"My mother, my mother! That was the final blow. I thought I could stand it…"

"I didn't know…" Franz said.

Hitler turned his white puffed face into Franz. His mouth reeked.

"She was murdered by a Jew!"

"She was?"

Franz said it with as much feeling as he could muster to conceal his contempt. Now the evidence was coming. He was beginning to see the bare outline of the future. This Austrian hick was preparing for revenge. The future would make perfect sense. Out of a life of poverty, indignity, failure, loss, rejection, homelessness, blind rage and hatred, this puny helpless fourth rate artist would transform himself into a murderer. And fate would make his sisters victims. There was no longer any doubt in his mind.

"Butchered by a Jewish doctor who told me she would get well. He mutilated her in the interest of science. My sainted mother!"

The dam broke and Hitler wept openly. It was an alley; they were alone. Dr. Kafka was understanding and respectable. One German to another. It was permissible.

"She died of Jewish meddling. They mutilated a pure German mother. I tell you I will build a monument to her over the graves of the Jewish butchers."

"During an operation?" Franz asked.

"Three of them! Three! Butchers! To think of what they did to the crown of motherhood! The source of life! The pillow of peace! The center of serenity! The core of being!"

Franz was on the verge of helpless laughter. Did they sew up her cunt? What was all this blather about? He now had to add stupidity and schmaltz to his list of Hitler's characteristics. He thought of his own mother, whom he found enslaved and pathetic. Where were Hitler's feelings coming from? What fictions had he invented that now appeared tragically real? Yes, this was funny. Decidedly funny.

Finally, Hitler said it. He forced it out of his mouth like some remaining undigested food. It sprang out at Franz.

"Cancer! Breast Cancer!" Hitler cried. "I will never forgive them!"

Them!

"I nursed her to the end. Alone. I watched her shrink and waste away and I asked God, Why? Why not my father who lived a long stupid life and died a powerful man, even in death."

Hitler sobbed into Franz's handkerchief.

"When I build my monument to her, no one will forget her!"

As he leaned over and retched pitifully, Franz's contempt grew.

Then, by an almost visible act of will, Hitler righted himself and placed his fists on his breast.

"The blood that flowed in my sacred mother's veins flows in mine. I am blood of her blood and I will revenge her, Dr. Kafka, sir."

His fists opened slowly and he lay his pale hands on Franz's coat. White scum had collected at the corners of his mouth. He smelled like a goat.

He became calmer. He put his hands down to his sides and he dropped his head so that Franz, taller than Hitler, was staring at the top of his head.

I could do it now, Franz thought. One blow with a blunt object would kill this weakling, this romantic crybaby, this maudlin hick and I could leave him in this alley to be collected like refuse. Or I could carry his body to the river and throw it in. They'd never find out who he is; no one in the world would claim him—this helpless, homeless, friendless reject.

When Hitler raised his head again, he was contrite.

"Excuse me, Dr. Kafka. I didn't mean... Something broke inside me..."

"I don't suppose you want to go back in," Franz said. "When the play ends, Zak does some songs and jokes."

"I think I'd better go," Hitler said.

"Let me walk with you a bit," Franz offered.

"Tha'd be helpful," Hitler said gratefully.

Chapter Fourteen

When Franz returned to the Café Savoy, he heard a piano and Zak's voice, but the audience and the rest of the troupe had gone. He was singing one of his familiar patter songs to Ottla:

> I'm Yitzak Levi, I ain't no heavy,
> I like to dance and joke and prance around and sing.
> I'm Yitzak Levi, a schlep from Schvevy,
> A crazy ghetto nut who wouldn't be a king!
>
> I have two buddies, they are not duddies,
> They love to come to see me act and dance and joke.
> One is called Franzi, one is called Ottla,
> They are the best of all the Czech and German folk!

As Franz listened and Ottla clapped her hands to the beat, he wondered if he could draw Zak into his scheme.

"Where's Alf?" Ottla asked when Zak had finished. "What was going on? All of a sudden he pops up and out he goes."

"He got sick," Franz said. "Must have been something he ate."

"Or saw," Zak said, making a face. "Was I *that* bad?"

"Where'd he go?" Ottla asked.

"He went back to the hostel."

"I hope he'll be all right," Ottla said. "I like him."

"A real Austrian charmer," Franz said with a sneer to Zak that passed right over Ottla's head.

"I'm jealous already," Zak said to Ottla. "You know why we're staying in Prague, don't you? The real reason.

Not for the audiences or the big money, it's because of you."

"Don't believe him," Franz said. "It's the bureaucracy."

"No, no," Zak protested. "I've never felt more at home in any other city."

"How sweet!" Ottla crooned. "I'll bet you say that to every city."

"What's with this Hootler guy? He doesn't seem to fit in."

"We just met," Ottla said. "And his name is Hitler."

"He's got a crush on Ottla," Franz said.

Ottla blushed.

"You don't like him?" Zak asked Franz.

"He brought him home," Ottla said defensively.

"I felt sorry for him," Franz said. "He looked like he needed a meal."

"That's not like you," Ottla said, "taking people off the streets." Then, addressing Zak, "My brother's a real loner. We get company, he walks out."

"Really? That's not the impression I get," Zak said.

"I'm changing," Franz said. "I'm beginning to see the importance of social intercourse."

Zak had begun to take off his makeup, and as Franz watched he was surprised to see a version of himself emerge—a smiling happier version. Like him, Zak was tall and thin and had a long face. He even had big ears. But his hair was different—light brown—and his eyes were blue. His face was lit by a continuous smile.

"So what's with..." Zak asked Ottla.

"Oh, he's cute, that's all."

"Cute?" Franz said distastefully. "That better be all. Anyway, he'll be leaving Prague soon."

"Is he?" she said with a frown.

"He's got enough sketches."

"No, he hasn't."

"Is he any good?" Zak asked.

Ottla said "Yes" as her brother said "No."

"He is, too," Ottla said. "He's very good."

"He's one of these deadeye realists," Franz mocked. "You know, one of those artists who says, 'There's a chair, I will draw it and it will look just like a chair.'"

"I don't believe this," Ottla said. "I thought you liked him."

"I've changed my mind."

"Well, I like him! What made you change your mind?"

"Our father," Franz lied.

"That figures," Ottla said to Zak. "Daddy likes Alf, so of course Franz has to hate him!"

"You've got good taste," Zak said to Franz. "Your father isn't the most likeable man in the world."

"And he falls all over a fourth rate artist," Franz said.

"Why are you doing this?" Ottla pleaded with her brother.

"I don't want to get involved in a family quarrel," Zak said, "so why don't we sing some songs?"

"Germans together!" Franz yodeled. "Empire supporters! Reich leaders! March! March! March! The postcard painter thinks we're Germans."

"Well, in a sense we are," Ottla said.

"Not in his sense," Franz went on, determined now to make some revelations. "He's a ferocious anti-Semite."

"He is not!"

"Worse than our father."

"Father's not an anti-Semite," Otlla said. "How can a Jew be an anti-Semite?"

"You're looking at one!" Franz shouted.

"Me, too," Zak said, biting his lip.

"How could that be?" Ottla demanded.

"I think you're being a little naïve, Ottla," Zak said.

"What do I have in common with Jews?" Franz said. "I hardly have anything in common with myself."

"Then what are we doing here?" Ottla said. "For months you've been dragging me around to all the Yiddish theater shows. Some anti-Semite you are!"

"I'm a Yiddish-loving anti-Semite Jew!"

Zak slapped a resolving chord on the piano.

"I know what he means," he said.

Ottla threw her hands up.

"I don't know what you're talking about!"

Franz reached over and touched her arm.

"My dearest sister, you've got a lot to learn."

"Oh, what's the difference," she said weakly, "as long as people like one another?"

"And what if they don't?" Franz said. "What then?"

Franz looked into his sister's dark eyes, wondering if now was the time to tell her, but Zak interrupted with an out-of-key version of his song:

> I have two buddies, they are not duddies,
> They love to come to hear me act and dance and joke.
> One is called Franzi! One is called Ottla!
> They are the very best of Czech and German folk!

"That's just it," Franz said. "What are we? Czech? German? Jew?"

"What does it matter," Ottla pleaded, "as long as we get along?"

"What happens when we don't get along anymore?" Franz said.

"What happens," Zak said with uncharacteristic seriousness, "when I can't get a permit anymore? I have to check in with the police and get a permit everywhere I go. And they look at me suspiciously and say, 'What kind of a language is Yiddish?' which sounds like 'What kind of disease have you got?' When my competitor, Zachariah Franzos started out with his Yiddish Art Theater, they asked him that question. You know what he would say? 'Oh, it's similar to German, or Hebrew, or French,' whoever he was talking to, trying to give himself respectability."

"It *is* respectable," Ottla protested. "I love it."

"But does your father? No. Most respectable Jews want to get far away from Yiddish and everyone connected to it. Yiddish reminds modern Jews of their past—all those funny-looking people in beards and caftans and ringlets who are so poor and clannish and smelly. We don't want to talk about our eastern brethren. Take my own mother and father. Two Hassidics. If they knew what I'm doing for a living, they'd keel over in their prayer shawls."

"I don't want to upset you, Ottla," Franz said, "but do you know what would happen if this Mr. Hitler…"

"Alf," Ottla corrected.

"…found out we were Jews?"

"Aha!" Zak cried. "The fog clears."

"No," Ottla said. "What would he do?"

"First of all, you'd never see him again."

"I don't believe that."

"Secondly, he would hate you. He'd think he was deceived and he'd make a little note in his fermented brain about his evil treatment at our hands."

"But you went to German school!" Ottla said. "We're Germans. We speak it. We live it."

"I, myself, am a citizen of the world," Zak said with a light touch. "I have friends in every city in Europe. All assimilated, of course."

Ottla looked from Zak to her brother, back and forth.

"I don't believe Alf would care. I can see it in his eyes, in his manners."

"Tell him, then," Franz challenged. "Tell him who we really are."

"What I don't understand," Zak said, "is how you know so much about him if he's only been here a few days."

"I drew him out."

"But why bother? What's in it for you? You'll never see this guy again once he leaves Prague."

"I'm collecting material for a story," Franz said.

That seemed to satisfy for the moment, but Franz read skepticism in Zak's eyes. Could he approach him later?

That evening, Franz wrote the following in his journal:

"My urge to depict my dreamlike inner life has thrust everything into the background. My fate is simple. I must write, and now I am compelled to act, yet my life dwindles dreadfully. I waver. I fly up, then I fall back again.

"The Thing is after me. Is it a dream within a dream? It goads me into action and once I act, I feel that I will have cast off incomprehensible burdens. And yet to act in this way fills me with terror. Can I trust another person? How will I explain myself? Dreams may be powerful, but they are singular. They happen only to individuals. The great dreamers of history are those who can convince others that their dreams are attainable. I have no ability to do that. I am not convinced by my own voice. My dreams compel me, but where? I feel that a great good will come of my action, but my skeptical mind broods and doubts."

Chapter Fifteen

Franz, Ottla, Alf, and Zak walked briskly over the Charles Bridge. They were on their way to an outing in the countryside on a beautiful day whose contradictions tore at Franz's heart. He concealed his feelings as usual, focussing on revelations from the artist-in-residence.

"Frankly," he said to Alf in a conversation he had begun about Wagner, "I can't tell the difference between *The Merry Widow* and *Tristan and Isolde*."

"I find that hard to believe," Hitler said.

"Some people just have no ear for music," Zak said.

Franz wiggled his ears and laughed.

"I should get some compensation for my ears," Zak said.

"What's wrong with *The Merry Widow*?" Ottla asked.

"Music requires emotional surrender," Franz said, "and I don't like to surrender."

"Surrender?" Zak said. "When I sing, people attack me!"

"It's not surrender," Hitler said. "You join in the vision of the heroic composer. You are swept to victory."

"To the illusion of victory," Franz corrected. "All you've done is given away your money to appear in a fantasy."

"Will somebody please tell me what's wrong with *The Merry Widow*?" Ottla asked, puffing to keep up with the men.

"Nothing," Zak said, "if you're a bourgeois chocolate-eater."

"Lehar, Strauss. Their music is warmed-over sentiment," Franz said.

They walked abreast, Ottla between Franz and Zak, Hitler next to Franz. He had tried to be Ottla's partner, but Zak the Yid, whom Hitler despised, cut him off. Franz saw it happen and knew just what Hitler was thinking from the venomous expression on his face.

At first, Hitler had refused to come along when he heard Zak would be a member of the party, but Ottla convinced him. She was growing fonder of the Austrian.

"When we get back," Franz said, "we'll take the boat out and have a swim in the river."

"I'm no swimmer," Hitler said. "I'll stay in the boat."

"You don't swim?" Ottla said. "We love to swim; we go all the time in the summer."

"I never learned," Hitler said. "There was no opportunity in my town."

"Where's that?" Zak asked.

"Outside of Linz. A small place."

"On the Danube?"

"Yes, but it's only a trickle there. I've always wanted to learn," Hitler explained, "especially after reading about the way American Indians can swim."

"We'll teach you, Alf," Ottla said.

"What about the American Indians?" Franz asked.

"In Karl May's novels. I've read them all. I still read them. They're all about livin' a basic, pure life in nature, close to the blood of the forefathers."

"Sounds just like my life in Warsaw," Zak said.

"You've never read them, of course," Hitler asked scornfully.

"Never heard of them," Zak said.

"Every German boy reads Karl May. I was in tears when Winnetou, the Indian chief, died in the arms of his old friend. My father found me cryin' and he asked what I was cryin' about, but I would never tell him. He didn't deserve to know. That was one of the few times I cried as a child."

"I don't think Karl May'll fit into the Yiddish Theater."

Franz laughed, but Hitler stared stonily ahead.

"This is fun," Ottla said, "but you're going too fast for me." The men slowed down a trifle. "I've never read a book about America."

"That's because you're too involved with that Girl's Club," Franz said.

"I am not!"

"You are, too. You go to more meetings than anybody I know."

"I want to be informed!"

"Yes," Franz said, watching Hitler, "but I don't want you going off to Palestine to live like a pioneer."

"What's wrong with that?" Ottla said. "And it's the Zionist Girls' and Women's Club!"

"Excuse me!"

"You're demeaning it by calling it only a girl's club."

"If Zionism's only for Jews…" Hitler began.

"I'm thinking about writing an article about this new fad," Franz said.

"New fad?" Ottla shouted.

"…and Ottla's helping me with the research."

"Have you heard about *The Protocols of the Wise Men of Zion*? Zak asked.

"What's that?" Ottla said.

"Plots. Jewish plots," Zak said. "To conquer the world."

"Don't even bother explaining it," Franz said.

"I'd like to hear about it," Hitler said.

"What's a protocol?" Ottla asked.

"It's a document," Franz said. "But let's forget about it and enjoy the day. It's all a fraud and invention, anyway. Like trying to go to Palestine and living in the desert. Try it sometime and see what you get. You're wasting your time."

"What do they say—these protocols?" Hitler asked.

"If we don't change the subject," Franz shouted, "I'm turning around and going back!"

They were in the Kleinseite now, walking through the trees and mounting the first hill.

"Franz is right," Zak said. "It's all a fraud. But some people are taking it seriously, anyway. I've heard about these protocols in every city I've been in." He took note of Franz's scowl. "All right, I'll shut up, but just let me say this: the whole idea of Jews running the world is funny to begin with. Of all people! Running the world! They've never stopped running, period! I think I'll write a song about it and sing it at the Savoy. Let's see, what rhymes with 'Zion'? Lion, frying, scion, buyin', pie-in... your face!"

"Can you just give me an idea...?" Hitler said.

"Why do you want to know?" Franz said. "Why does a good German want to know about some demented, half-baked scheme? It's a fraud. Why spread lies? Let's just forget about it!"

"Is there any connection...?" Hitler began.

"Between what?" Zak asked.

"That these documents appear at the same time Zionism does?"

"There's *no* connection," Franz said, completely exasperated. "There's no cause and effect. One is a ridiculous lie and the other is a utopian dream. It's all bullshit!"

"Franz!" Ottla said.

"Well, it is!"

"What are you getting all excited about? All Alf wants is to talk about it."

Ottla's defense of Hitler was the last straw. Franz swung around and headed back toward the bridge.

"I don't want to walk anymore. I'm going to the boat. I'll meet you there later."

The trio—Ottla, Zak, Hitler—was stunned by Franz's outburst. With varied reactions, they watched him march off. Had they been able to see Franz's expression, they would have noticed a leer cross his face.

Chapter Sixteen

There was no fog on the river; Franz could see for miles around. The castle on the hill seemed a stone's throw away. It loomed out of all proportion to its importance.

He rowed his little boat, condemning himself for his foolish behavior. He was sure that Hitler knew now. He didn't know if his slip-up, conscious or not, had been a wise thing. What was going on in Hitler's mind now, he wondered, as he tramped through the woods with a little Jewish girl and a self-professed Yid?

How stupid of him to leave like that, but he had been close to being caught and his instinct was, as always, to get out. It was similar to so many situations he found himself in—similar to what happened in Dr. Pribram's office, what happened in his home, what happened in his head. It was always the same: a loss of control, a sort of self-condemnation, a trap he permitted himself to spring on himself. Outrageous and stupid! And still he hadn't written the letter to Dr. Pribram. Had Karl made an attempt at it yet? God, what confusion! It filled his private life, his business life, his journals and his stories.

Prior to that fateful dream, his misery was internal, family-oriented. Suddenly now, his father was not the only ogre in his life. Suppose Hitler panicked and carried out his plan now? He saw his dear Ottla fall under Hitler's blows. Zak came to her defense, but Zak fell, too.

Franz stopped rowing, pulled his oars in and covered his face with his hands, trying to obliterate the very images his mind was speedily creating.

A violent shaking of the dinghy caused him to fling his arms apart and grab the sides of the boat. There, in front of him again, was the miserable Golem—ugly, frightening, his teeth bared in that perpetually angry expression. There was a yellow star on his breast.

"Hello, again, Man of Destiny," the Golem said sardonically. "Now you've put your foot in it! And you'll continue to make a mess of things until you *do* something!"

"You!" Franz whined.

"It wasn't too smart of you to leave them alone."

"I know, I just realized it," Franz said.

"I wouldn't be too worried about it," the Golem said. "He's after more than two."

"What do you mean?"

"Two don't a pogrom make."

"A pogrom!"

"What do you think it's gonna be? A fancy dress ball?"

"I… I have no taste for this. I'm not a murderer. The man may be vile, but that doesn't mean…" Franz shook his head. "It's too much for me."

"The fear you have for your sister right now," the Golem said. "Multiply it, multiply it many times, over and over. Imagine the worst."

"I can't."

"You mean you won't! Don't hide your head in the sand. You're a writer, a lawyer. Imagine it!"

"No."

"You must!"

"I can't!"

The Golem reached out and grabbed Franz's coat. He pulled him forward until their faces were only inches apart.

"Come on, you Yiddish-loving anti-Semite Jew bastard! You alienated intellectual! You miserable narcissist!"

"That's my phrase!" Franz said.

113

"And I've heard it, I've heard all of your excuses, your woeful rationalizations, your delay, your self-pity. I'm throwing them right back in your face!"

The Golem released him and Franz fell back heavily. The rocking boat took on water.

"Making fun of Zionism! The only real answer we have! Do you think anybody is going to treat us right until we demand it!?"

"I hate all of this."

"That's not what you said to Irma Singer."

"Irma Singer? What did I say to Irma Singer?"

"Convenient forgetfulness! You don't remember questioning her—in detail—about life in Palestine? After everybody else had moved onto other subjects? You don't remember what you wrote in her book?"

"What did I write?" Franz asked, "And how would you know?"

"You wrote: 'I'm not healthy enough to see things your way.' Isn't that so? You admitted your sickness and inferiority. You're not good enough to be a Zionist! That's your self-pity! Do you want to perish along with your sisters?"

"Stop!" Franz shrieked, slapping his hands to his face. "Stop tormenting me!"

As the dinghy shook again, he looked up and saw that the Golem had vanished once more. The river was calm, Prague glistened in the distance, and somewhere in the hills the destroyer of his sister accompanied her.

But why, Franz wondered, why is Hitler going to destroy his sisters? He was clearly enamored of Ottla. Was the dream incomplete?

The nightmare he was living through was made worse by his endless examination of the countless questions that struck his brain like knives. If only he could act blindly, in total obedience to the will of his dream!

He saw Ottla fall, fatally injured (how? by what weapon?), then Valli, then Elli, their faces bloody, their mouths distorted by shrieks. Yes, he would have to do it, he would have to find a way. When Ottla and Zak returned with him to the river, he'd invite them all in for a row. The dinghy being too small for the four of them, he'd suggest that Zak take Ottla out and when they returned, he would go out with Hitler... who cannot swim.

He'd row out to the deepest part of the river (at the point he had in mind, ten feet or more), and then, making it seem an accident, pitch the boat over and let him drown. It would be over quickly. His sisters would be safe and he would take courage in the knowledge that he had saved them.

But still the question why obsessed him. Because they were Jews? Even so, why not three Jewish women of Vienna? Or Berlin? Or Munich?

And then the Golem's word struck him. A pogrom! There was going to be a pogrom, and in that case, many were going to be destroyed. The dream didn't reveal that. Nor was it clear what that machine was that made the horrible noise in the street.

Franz fought and wrestled with himself for another hour, and then he heard the hail of voices from the shore. All three of them were waving vigorously. They looked like comrades. From this distance, he could hardly tell them apart.

He rowed in and confronted an enthusiastic trio. Hitler had his arm around Ottla.

"We had a wonderful walk!" Ottla said. "You missed it!"

"Exhilaratin'," Hitler said.

"I got blisters from it," Zak complained.

"You're a slowpoke," Ottla said. "We left you in the dust."

"They did," Zak admitted.

"You owe her a row, then, Zak," Franz said.

"I'll go out with Ottla," Hitler said escorting her to the dinghy.

"Why don't we all go?" Zak said.

"It won't take four," Franz said.

"You and Zak go after us," Ottla said.

She was defying her brother. In this matter, she could not be allowed to succeed.

"No!" Franz commanded. "Zak and Ottla go. Alf can't swim so he'd better go with me."

Hitler's face became rigid. He released Ottla who grudgingly boarded the dinghy with Zak as Franz got out.

"No use taking chances," Franz said.

"Oh, nothing would happen," Ottla whined.

"It's *my* boat! I'm the captain! You can't be too careful on the river."

Zak took the oars as Franz pushed them out. Zak sang:

"And then he'd row, row, row,

Straight up the river he would row, row, row…"

Hitler's face was cramped with anger, but he said nothing.

"What's the matter?" Franz said, as they watched them head out.

"Nothing." Hitler said.

"I thought you had a good time."

"We did."

"It won't take four," Franz shrugged.

"I know."

"Don't you like Zak?"

"I didn't care for his acting," he said.

"Be honest. You don't like him, do you?"

"Not really…"

"Because he's a Jew?"

"I never said that."

"But that's how you feel."

Hitler looked up at the taller man abjectly.

"Dr. Kafka… I…"

"Don't you think it's time to be getting back to Vienna? You've got your sketches, haven't you?"

"Some of them," Hitler said, looking out on the river.

"You like Ottla, don't you?"

Hitler, blinking rapidly, said nothing.

"She's just a kid, you know," Franz said.

Hitler remained silent, his eyes averted. That was the end of their talk.

They sat on the narrow shoreline and observed the tiny, undefined figures in the boat.

After a long silence, Franz said, "Who is this Karl May you were talking about? I've never heard of him."

Hitler stirred himself to enthusiasm.

"I told you, every German boy reads him."

"Not *every*," Franz said.

"Real Germans do. The first one was *The Ride Through The Desert*. I read every one after that. I paid no attention to school. My father got after me, but I didn't care. My mother said, 'Let the boy read.'… I found out that Karl May once actually lived in Linz. For almost a year, he lived in a hotel on the Danube. Some day I'm going to build a monument to him in the town square."

"And these were all Indian stories?"

117

"Not all of them. They took place all over the world—even Siberia. But the greatest are the Indian tales of the wild west. Especially *Winnetou*. Old Shatterhand is a German immigrant who teams up with Winnetou. He learns all the Indian's tricks and become a leader. He tames wild horses, strangles wild beasts with his bare hands, defeats other Indians in knife-fights, leads armies..."

"Fantasy literature," Franz said.

"No!" Hitler said sharply. "No! Heroic literature, to build your hopes and dreams and morale. When Winnetou dies, he gives old Shatterhand the charm he's worn all his life to ward off evil and bring good luck."

Hitler opened his shirt and pulled a medallion into view.

"I found this in a shop in Vienna and I've worn it ever since."

"Isn't that a Buddhist charm?" Franz said.

"No, no," Hitler corrected. "It's Winnetou's."

It looked like this:

"So I guess you'd recommend Karl May," Franz said indifferently.

"More than any other writer."

The man's a boor, Franz thought, but he's still better off than the unfortunate creature I am.

Chapter Seventeen

The sun was low when Ottla and Zak returned. They got out of the boat noisily, full of talk and cheer. Hitler looked envious and withdrawn. And now he had to set off with the eminent Dr. Kafka!

Franz rowed earnestly, aiming for the deepest part of the river, wanting to get well out of sight of Zak and Ottla.

They faced each other, Hitler with his hands grasping the sides of the dinghy, Franz hitting the water with regular strokes.

"Great exercise," Franz said.

"You do it well," Hitler said.

"This is my favorite sport."

"The sun's going down," Hitler said.

"Don't worry," Franz said, "I know this river. We'll get back by the last light."

He rowed along the green banks to the spot where the Golem had first appeared. The banks had been fogged-in on that day; now there was a crystal clarity all around. The sunset was brilliant, the river was a glassy dark blue.

Franz pulled in the oars.

"Would you like to try?" he asked Hitler.

"No." Hitler was firm about it.

"It's really very easy."

"I'll just sit."

"I had a visit here one day," Franz said.

"A visit? From who?"

"The Golem."

"The Golem?"

"Not too long ago."

"The Golem you were tellin' me about?"

119

"None other. I was sitting where you are now, dozing off, when all of a sudden the boat started shaking from side to side, like this…"

Franz raised himself and rocked his body from one side to the other in quick abrupt gestures that caused Hitler to release his grip. Then Franz put his foot next to the oarlock, jammed it down, and capsized the boat. He threw himself clear of the dinghy and felt the shock of the cool river. He thought he had heard a yelp from Hitler before going under.

When he surfaced, ten yards away, there was no sign of him. Then he heard a hollow squealing coming from under the capsized boat and realized Hitler had been caught there.

"Alf! Alf!" he called, for proper effect. "Where are you?"

He did not swim from his position. He made some splashing motions and uttered a few more cries before submerging himself as if he were drowning. When he came up, he saw that Hitler had somehow got out from under the dinghy and he was retching for air in the panicky way non-swimmers do. He was causing a gross disturbance in the otherwise tranquil river.

The current had caused the boat to wander away so there was no chance that Hitler could grab onto it. Franz submerged again, stayed down for a few moments, came up with more impotent cries of help, and could not have heard the splash by the shore, nor seen a passerby pointing emphatically. Soon, however, he saw a swimmer streaking towards the flailing man, and Franz then realized his plan was going to be thwarted.

There was great turmoil along the shore, great confusion, shouts, tears, weeping, self-reproaches, ghastly stories, heroic tales of salvation.

They hired a carriage to carry Hitler and themselves to the Kafka's. They burst in upon the mother and father dramatically. There were breathless explanations, breathless responses; there were tears.

"Who saved him?" Hermann Kafka demanded to know.

"A man by the name of Viktor Adler," Ottla said.

"What luck! Did you thank him? Did you…?"

"Oh, yes," Zak said. "A hundred times."

"The man's a hero," Hermann Kafka said. "Did you get his address?"

Zak said no; he asked Franz if he did.

"How could you expect him to get his address in *his* condition?" Hermann Kafka cried. "You should have used your noodle, Mr. Actor!"

"Who could think straight?" Ottla said.

"And what happened to you, Mr. Swimmer?" the father asked the son.

"The boat must have grazed my head as it capsized. I went under."

"How many times have I told you to be more careful, Mr. Swimmer and Rower. Do you realized what could have happened?"

The drama went on for most of the night, Hitler at the center of it, the happy survivor, pleased by the attentions of Ottla and her parents. Franz and Zak were exiled to the edges of the festivities and the stories that developed in greater and greater detail as the hours went by.

Helpless, Franz watched Ottla cater to Hitler, wipe his near-victim's brow, offer him drink and food, clear the table of his refuse. Zak, probably dismayed by his multiple defeats, left as early as good taste would permit. Mr. Kafka was happy to see him go and pulled no punches in saying so.

"I don't want that low-brow in my house anymore," he ordered. "And Ottla, you stay away from him!"

"He had nothing to do with any of this," Franz said.

"I don't care," Hermann Kafka thundered. "He's trouble wherever he goes!"

"How would you know?" Franz said.

"I know! I know! I know his type. I don't want my daughter in his company!"

Franz knew Hitler was lighting up inside, even though he saw no outward signs. He was too smart to show outwards signs!

Infuriated, Franz put himself in his room for the rest of the night. Let the *messhugeneh* Holy Family piously enjoy itself! Let the idiots, excepting his sister (although he was losing his patience with her, too), drown in their self-deceptions.

He was depressed. He felt black. What now? What now? Viktor Adler! Hero! Who could have imagined that a passerby…! That's why he waited till dusk. But that didn't stop Viktor Adler, whoever he was. It didn't stop that fool from interfering with destiny. Everything has gone wrong and now he had a suspicious Hitler on his hands. He was more endeared to his family than ever before, and was being given a bed, not thirty feet from Ottla's!

Chapter Eighteen

He stayed home the next day, sent a message to his office saying he was ill, and confined himself to his room. Since Ottla and his parents were at the store, Hitler had the run of the house. What diabolical irony! Few words passed between them. Franz saw Hitler only when he was getting something to eat. The intruder was at the kitchen table, trying to look scholarly and disciplined, working on his miserable sketches.

Franz wrote in his journal, poured his frustration and misery onto the pages. Then he paced his room, trying to conceive of his next step. He thought of getting dressed and going to see Max, or Zak, or Oskar—anyone—to tell the *whole* story, from beginning to end, leaving nothing out, begging for their assistance. But his will flagged when he realized what he would have to communicate. And even if they did accept his story—the whole story—which was improbable, would they collaborate in murder?

So he must be alone. Nothing new.

The artist Peter Ascher had once asked him to pose for a painting of St. Sebastian because he said Franz had the right physique for it, but now he knew Ascher's insight was deeper than that. He had the right *soul* for it! He was going to be a silent martyr for a great act—saving his sisters. And as soon as he had done it, he would get in touch with Peter so that he could paint the face and form of a murderer as one of Christianity's great martyrs!

That evening, he did not eat with his family and their guest. He kept himself away, brooding and thinking. Irritated by his son's attitude, Hermann Kafka wanted to know which one of them it was who came near to drowning. Why was the difficult Kafka son under the weather when the one who came closest to death was so hale and hearty?

Franz went to work the next day, but left early as a result of extreme indisposition. He hurried home, still arguing with himself. As he entered the apartment, he heard hasty sounds that made him suspicious. Hitler had the look of a cornered animal.

"Home so soon?" he asked weakly.

"I don't feel well," Franz said, looking around. "Who else is here?"

And then Ottla appeared. She had been hiding in the dining room and now she emerged reluctantly, as if she were being pushed into the open while another force, in front of her, resisted.

"I came home to get something for Momma and Poppa," Ottla said uneasily. "I just got here and I'm leaving now."

"Wait a minute," Franz said. "What is this?"

"Nothin'," Hitler said, crossing between them. "Nothin' at all."

"What's that?" Franz asked, pointing at Ottla's chest. "What's that around your neck?"

Ottla's fist enclosed the trinket Hitler had shown to Franz.

"Alf gave it to me," she said.

"Did he now? And what was the occasion?"

"It was a gift, Dr. Kafka," Hitler said. "Please do not assume anything. I am very fond of your dau... your sister."

"Take it off," Franz ordered his sister.

Ottla quickly pulled it over her head.

"Give it back to him."

Ottla did so. Hitler held the charm aloft, as if to offer it as a peace gesture. The emblem spun playfully.

"Dr. Kafka, Ottla and I…"

"Do you realize," Franz shouted, "that you are giving gifts to a Jewess? Do you realize that you have been eating the food of Jews? Do you realize that you have been sleeping in a Jewish bed? Are you aware that you have been living with Jews and are surrounded by Jews?"

As Hitler stepped backwards, his mouth fallen open, he put the charm in his pocket.

"Well, do you?" Franz demanded to know.

"Dr. Kafka, I…"

"Yes. Dr. Kafka. that's who I am, but a Jewish Dr. Kafka. Jews! All Jews!"

Franz turned to his sister.

"Go back to the store, Ottla! Say nothing of this to Mother and Father. Nothing! Do you hear me?"

"Yes, Franz," Ottla said, going to the door. "I'm sorry," she sniffed. She glanced hastily at Hitler. "I'm sorry."

Franz tried staring Hitler down, but his face had turned hard.

"So, now, how do you feel about your budding love affair with a Jewess?"

"She finds me… your sister is attracted to me," Hitler said.

"Really? But what about you? Touching all this filth? Living with this vermin?"

Hitler, suddenly, seemed revitalized. He stepped toward Franz.

"I felt it! I actually felt it! I'm not surprised. But your father…"

125

"You mean *Zugführer* Kafka of the German Army? A Jew! A better faker than you are. My father knows how to conceal an identity."

"He fooled me."

"He fools himself. He turned us all into anti-Semites. That's why you couldn't tell."

Hitler made a fist to accompany his rage.

"It wasn't an accident in the boat!"

"No," Franz said, shaking. "If it weren't for Viktor Adler, you'd be dead!"

"But why? Why did you try to kill me? What have I done to you? I never saw you before that day in the street."

"It's a matter of destiny," Franz said.

"Destiny?"

"It's beyond explanation now."

Hitler backed away. He moved into the kitchen.

"Who are you? What do you want with me?"

"You're a threat to my family. You're going to destroy them."

"Me? But they've treated me well."

"But now you know they're Jews, the vermin corrupting Germany."

"You don't know what you're talking about? I'm an artist; I'm a painter."

"And I'm an insurance man," Franz said.

They were in the kitchen now, coming face to face, when Hitler darted toward a draw, opened it, and pulled out a knife. It was the same knife Franz had used to protect his sisters in his first dream. He saw the man again, dismounting the machine and entering the house with the large package.

"Stay away," Hitler said, holding the knife out at the level of Franz's chest. "I want to build and create."

"Something's going to change all that."

"What?" Hitler cried. "What could it possibly be?"

"I've watched you; I've heard you," Franz said. "In the Arco, on the streets, in the theater. Don't you listen to yourself? Behind your pathetic mask is a hater, a vile and violent hater."

"I've got no mask," Hitler said. "I'm poor, I'm alone. All I want…"

As Hitler backed into the dining room, he passed into the arms of the Golem, who now had the six-pointed yellow star on his forehead. He crushed Hitler's chest. The knife dropped to the floor. Looking up and seeing the Golem's face, Hitler pulled his charm out of his pocket and held it up. The Golem cried out. It was a long, piercing, pitiful scream. He tightened his suffocating grip of Hitler's chest and raised one arm to put a lock on his neck.

"Go to the kitchen, turn on the oven, and leave," the Golem ordered Franz. "You botched one job."

"The oven?" Franz said.

"Yes. Turn it on full and then go to work. Tell your sister and parents that you convinced him to go back to Vienna. I'll dispose of the body."

"I tried my best," Franz said. "I tried."

The Golem motioned him to get out and as he pulled Hitler into the kitchen, the charm fell to the floor.

Chapter Nineteen

He walked to work in a trance. He told his surprised secretary that even though he wasn't feeling well, he had to finish some important work and he was not to be disturbed.

On his desk was Karl Blau's draft of the letter of apology to Dr. Pribram. It was no longer a matter of concern to Franz. Karl had phrased it well enough. He had mentioned Franz's well-known physical ailments. Then Franz had some new thoughts. Why should he accept total blame when both of them had made the fiasco happen? Franz took a box of matches out of a drawer, lit one, and set fire to the letter. He let it burn in his hand before dropping it in the waste basket. He felt the matter was ended.

He got up and went to a small room off his office in which he kept a cot. When he worked long hours and became fatigued, he often took a nap to refresh himself. He took his coat off, lay down, and in a few minutes he was asleep. And then he dreamed. A fire had broken out in his house. Fortunately, nobody was home. The blaze was confined to the Kafka residence; it did not spread. Franz thought of all his books and stories and journals that would soon be ashes. He wasn't concerned. His sisters were safe and that calmed all his usual anxieties. It was a very fine feeling. Out of that dream came a second: a piece of paper was burning. On it were printed the words he had written in his journal not two weeks before, after he had attended his nephew's circumcision:

I saw Western European Judaism before me in a transition whose end is clearly unpredictable and about which those most closely affected are not concerned, but, like all people in transition, bear what is imposed upon them.

As the paper was consumed, a beautiful scene appeared. It was a sunny day by the ocean and he was sitting on a lawn overlooking the sea. It was an immaculate moment. Large trees and pines provided shade. Flowers bloomed in sun-filled beds. And, best of all, people were sitting on the lawn, chatting and laughing and singing. They were led by Yitzak Levi, the happiest of them all, who played a piano and sang the sweetest. Ottla sat next to him, more beautiful than she ever looked, and Elli and Valli and their husbands and children were close by. Hermann and Julie Kafka were there, too, proud parents and grandparents, keeping time to Yitzak's music.

Chapter Twenty

A month later, Franz wrote the following in his journal.

My sisters are now safe. I feel it. The memory of that dream no longer haunts me. I have discovered that action is another kind of ax to break the frozen flood within me. What price I will ultimately have to pay for what I have done I do not know. Whatever it is, I'm willing to pay it. In the meantime, I grow content. I do not feel cold anymore. The once-frozen waters are moving and life is pulsing within me. I have been going to the factory three times a week without complaint. I see my father aging and feel a need to help him. I also have been thinking about marriage more seriously than ever before. I'm supposed to meet some people from Berlin at Max's tomorrow night and I actually look forward to it. As for writing, I've been thinking of doing some material for Zak's theater— maybe a play or a farce. I've thought about the Golem many times, but he no longer troubles me. I'm going to ask Zak if he'd be interested in a skit or two with the Golem as the leading character. H. no longer comes up in conversation. Ottla and my father missed him for a week or so, then he dropped from their thoughts. They had been upset by his sudden departure, but I explained that artists are notorious in such matters, self-indulgent and narcissistic. I feel better than I have in years. For the first time in my life, I look forward to the years ahead of me and I see no reason why they can't be satisfying. I'll be thirty next year. Add forty to that—not too much to ask—and I'll have made it to 1953, past the half century mark. I see good times ahead. Between now and then, I'll marry, have children, and see the world. Writing will be my hobby, a personal delight and entertaining sideline. Ottla will marry and together we'll watch our beautiful children grow up.

No more bad dreams. They have vanished. In fact, I've been having happy and pleasant ones. In a recent one, Ottla and I and our spouses went touring through Germany. It was 1943. We were well-received in all the cities and spas we visited. The number of Jews living in Germany had increased markedly. This development was directly attributable to the law passed by the benevolent Meinecke government which had developed many wise policies. One of the best was to encourage the Jews of central and eastern Europe to settle in Germany until they regained their homeland. In this way, Germany fulfilled the fondest hopes of the Enlightenment. Germany has given the world great art, and now great statesmanship. We were so impressed by German hospitality that we were planning to move our families to Berlin.

FIN

About the Author

August Franza is a novelist, playwright, collagist, poet, short story writer who has been steadily producing creative work for forty years.

Three one-act plays have been produced at SUNY Stony Brook, Long Island, and at the late lamented Village Gate in New York City.

His collages have been exhibited at Generator Gallery in the East Village of New York City, in a Sag Harbor Art Gallery and at the Islip Arts Museum.

His essays, short stories, and poems have appeared in such diverse publications as *The New York Times*, *Newsday*, *Harvard Magazine*, *ETC: The Journal of Semantics*, *Commonweal*, *The English Journal*, *Harper's Magazine*, *Long Island Quarterly* and *Hampton Shorts*, an annual Long Island anthology of stories, essays, and poetry.

Eight chapbooks of poems have been published dealing (deliciously) with his wide travels, and, most recently, two short stories have appeared in *Hampton Shorts*. *Eagle Eye*, a short story drawn from an unpublished novel, was one of six finalists in a *Newsday* historical short story contest, which had over 400 submissions.

Two textbooks have been in print and have been selling for over a decade.

His degrees are from Brooklyn College (B.A.), Columbia University (M.A.), and SUNY, Stony Brook (Ph.D.) His dissertation, *THE FALLEN IDOL*, is about the relationship between the critic John Ruskin and the painter J.M.W. Turner.

Printed in the United States
5215

9 780759 680586